WHITE CLIFFS OF DOVER

WHITE CLIFFS OF DOVER

*An English Historical
World War II Novel*

The Third of the Claybourne Trilogy

MARY CHRISTIAN PAYNE

Published by TCK Publishing
www.TCKPublishing.com

**Sign up for the newsletter to get news, updates
and new release info from Mary Christian Payne:**
http://bit.ly/MaryChristianPayne

To 'Pale Feather', who inspires me, with love and gratitude.

1

It took five arduous years for Lily Claybourne to reach her goal. Five years with little sleep, continual attention to medical textbooks, laboratory experimentation and actual in-hospital training. With a single-minded determination, she plowed ahead, and finally, in June of 1925, she heard the coveted words she'd dreamed of since she was a small child. When the Dean of the London Medical School for Women called out her name, Lily proudly walked across the stage in the school auditorium and accepted her diploma. How odd it was to hear oneself referred to as "Doctor Lily Claybourne". Those two small letters in front of her name represented a watershed moment. From that time on, everything in her life would be measured by a different yardstick – before and after medical school. But June 1925 represented even more than that to Lily. It meant the end of the separation from her husband, Kit Claybourne. If she had been asked in 1920, when she'd left Claybourne Court after only fourteen months of marriage, she undoubtedly would have said that the marriage was over. Now, after such a prolonged period, it was no longer so black and white. That she still loved Kit was a given, and she knew he loved her as well. Love had never been an issue. But she'd learned they were so vastly different, in so many ways, and she couldn't imagine either of them changing enough to enable a resumption of the marriage. And yet...

The Christmas before her graduation in 1925, Kit brought Win, his son by his first wife, Eleanor, to London for the holiday. Win was ten years old by then. Pia Claybourne, Kit's daughter by an Italian woman whom he'd met on a holiday from Oxford when only eighteen, had been with Lily from the beginning of her journey. She'd completed her schooling at a wonderful girls' school in London. She'd then moved on to an excellent finishing school in Lausanne, Switzerland, Chateau Mont Choisi. She would be completing two years there in May, 1926. She, too, made the trip from Switzerland to London, to be with her family on that Christmas holiday. It was the first time the entire family had been gathered together since Lily had left Kit five years before. There had been no overt animosity during the time Kit and Lily were separated – they saw one another occasionally and there was always civility.

Lily had certainly never envisioned the breakdown of her marriage after only fourteen months. She'd truly meant the vows she'd taken – to love one another until death parted them. But, in Lily's mind, death *had* parted them. Death of respect, death of the ability to communicate, the unnecessary death of a child due to Typhoid Fever that might have been avoided… and, perhaps most profoundly, the death of Kit and Lily's unborn baby. Too much sorrow. The deeper issues affecting the couple were their total lack of capacity to work out the differences that existed regarding major viewpoints. Kit was a strict traditionalist, as his family before him had been. Lily, on the other hand, took a modernist view of life and embraced the changes that society was facing at the end of the Great War in 1918. Kit couldn't imagine a woman ever wanting to be a physician. He wanted a wife who would be fulfilled by playing the role of countess to his earl. She wanted more than to be an ornament on his arm for the rest of her life. Lily had an enormous capacity to love and to care about the welfare of others. She was exceptionally bright and had dreamed of practicing medicine since trailing around behind her physician father when only a small child. Her parents had encouraged her goals.

Kit had lost his father at a relatively young age, in his twenties, and from that time forward, as the Earl of Gloucester, he had been consumed with the responsibilities that such a title implies. He oversaw an estate of immense proportions, some three thousand acres, and was the steward of the legacy that had fallen to him upon his father's death. All of his life he had been taught that the primary thing was to honor and protect the name of Claybourne. For the most part, that meant following the old ways and adhering to past traditions. With such vastly different viewpoints it had been inevitable that sooner or later there would be a clash. Kit expected an easily molded, submissive wife, and Lily wanted a full partnership. It was almost bound to fail.

But, love still remained. They both respected the other and didn't want a life with anyone else. In each heart was the spark of hope that a solution might be found and the marriage saved. Lily hadn't spent a lot of time thinking about such things during the preceding five years, as medical school had been all-consuming. But, graduation was looming in six months, and she knew that it was time for her to make a final decision. Would they try to put the marriage back together, or admit that they had failed and forever sever all ties?

They both knew that a long-overdue talk needed to take place during the upcoming Christmas holiday. After Kit's arrival in London, he immediately went out and purchased a gorgeous fir tree that was erected in the drawing room at their London home. He'd brought boxes of ornaments from Claybourne Court, so he and the children set about decorating it. Lily was finishing up at the hospital before her long-anticipated winter break.

She was a bit surprised when she saw Kit doing so many things himself, without asking for help from any of the servants. He even built the fire in the drawing room. Lily could remember   suggesting just that sort of thing when they'd first married, and he'd been appalled at the idea that one could live without a full staff of people serving his every need. Lily was a bit confused and couldn't decide if he was trying to impress her, or if a change in outlook had really occurred. Kit even took care of all the gift shopping, since Lily was still so immersed with medical study. She had to admit that he did a splendid job of it.

When Christmas Eve arrived, the family attended services at Westminster Abbey. It was a lovely, meaningful service. When leaving the church at midnight, it had just begun to snow. Great, thick white flakes fell. There was no wind, and nothing stirred. The church bells rang in the distance as they made their way back to their lovely home with its welcoming fire. Kit was strolling next to Lily, and the two children were behind them. Without any drama, Kit took his wife's hand as they walked together silently. It seemed very natural and right. When they reached the house, after shedding coats and boots, Kit made a wonderful eggnog spiced with rum. Then they set about opening gifts. It was clear from the beginning that Kit had outdone himself. Pia was delighted with many new articles of clothing, and Win, whose latest passion was airplanes, received everything from models that he could put together himself, to perfect replicas constructed of metal and designed so that even the tiny propellers turned. Kit was practical with Lily, giving her a fully equipped leather physician's bag and a lovely calfskin attaché case.

When the unwrapping was complete, the young people busied themselves with gifts, and Kit opened a bottle of champagne. Eventually Win and Pia drifted off to bed, kissing their parents and thanking them for a perfect Christmas. They were finally alone for one of the few times since they'd parted nearly five years before. He sat down at her feet, while she made herself comfortable on the drawing room sofa. Not being used to drinking alcohol, Lily felt a bit tipsy, but it was nice to be able to relax and let go. She felt happy and fulfilled. There was silence in the room for a few moments, but neither felt uncomfortable. It was pleasant to have the peace of the fire, a glass of fine champagne and the closeness of one another. Finally Kit spoke.

"Lily, now that you're coming to the end of this long journey, what are your feelings? Have you given any thought to what you want to do after completing your training?"

"Of course I've thought about my plans, Kit. I've thought about them during this entire period, but certainly much more of late when I know the end is upon me."

"And have you reached any conclusions?" he asked.

"Oh, Kit. Some days I'm certain that I want to return to Claybourne-on-Colne and go into practice with John. He's made me a wonderful offer. He says that I can take over the part of his practice that deals exclusively with women – obstetrics, gynecology and the like. Also, he would add the pediatric patients to my load, so that I'd virtually see my patients from before they're born until they leave childhood. He feels that all of his female patients would be thrilled to have a woman caring for them. I'd be the first woman doctor in the entire Gloucestershire area. He's also agreed that I can do whatever I want with my portion of the practice, including devoting a day or two a week to giving free care to those who can't afford to pay. It's truly ideal."

"It does sound wonderful. Why are you questioning the offer?"

"Kit, you know as well as I that it would be impossible for me to return to Claybourne-on-Colne and not also return to being the Countess of Gloucester. It would never do. It would be difficult for you, and it would be for me as well. So, while I do love the idea of practicing with John, there are other considerations."

John Garrett was the physician she had worked with when she'd volunteered for the Voluntary Aid Detachment during the Great War. They had been stationed at the same field hospital in France. He was also a close friend to Kit. They had known one another since Sandhurst Military College. After the war he and his wife, Gena, who had also nursed with Lily in France, had settled in Claybourne-on-Colne, and John had established a successful medical surgery in that small village. Now Lily had the opportunity to go into partnership with him.

Kit stood and returned with another bottle of champagne. Lily knew she'd reached her limit, but it was such a lovely night and she didn't have any responsibilities the next day. So, throwing caution to the wind, she accepted another glass. He sat down on the sofa beside her.

"Lily, you know how I've always felt about you. Nothing has changed in that regard. I'd love nothing better than for you to return to Claybourne Court and see if we can put our marriage back together."

"I'd like that too, Kit, but I'm worried. I'm not certain how much has changed. I've seen a difference in you, and I certainly know that I've grown enormously, but there are matters that need to be discussed. I've been so hesitant to get into all of this."

"I think they must be discussed, Lily. You'll be graduating soon, and decisions have to be made. You're right when you say I've changed. Five years has been a long time to think, to talk to others, and to sort out my feelings. I've spent an enormous amount of time doing that."

"So have I, Kit. When I haven't been memorizing diseases," she laughed. "I can tell you this much. I know now that I, too, made a lot of mistakes. I don't think I should have married you so quickly after returning from

France. I'm not certain we knew one another well enough. You thought you knew me, and I thought I knew you. But the truth is, we'd spent very little actual time together, and had never really discussed values and expectations. I've mellowed a lot. I had a burning desire to fulfill myself. Well, I've done that. And it was very, very difficult. I'm not as eager to change the world as I once was. I still have a great desire to help others, and to do good for people less fortunate than I, but I also understand that there is a place for tradition in the world. Tradition is a beautiful thing when loo ked at in the proper way. Now I have a much better understanding about why your mother became so upset when I didn't consult her about the changes I made at Claybourne Court. That was wrong of me. I can be headstrong at times. As far as things of an intimate nature, we should have worked harder at understanding each other's needs, as well as our vastly different upbringings and views on life. I'd grown accustomed to being independent when I returned from France. I'm not certain I was ready to share my life. On the other hand, I don't think you were either. You were running away, trying to turn a page without fully studying the impact that Eleanor had upon you. You had some terribly rigid views that I could never have adopted, such as not letting me carry money of my own and telling me how I should wear my hair."

"I know, Lily, I know. I've had a lot of time to think about those things. On top of that, I've had numerous talks with John. He's been wonderful. It's helped me to secure the viewpoint of someone who knows both of us. He and Gena have a solid marriage, and he's helped me to understand that sort of thing doesn't just happen without a lot of give and take. Lily, if we were to re-do our wedding trip, I can tell you unequivocally, nothing would be the same. Of course we'd go sightseeing. That was abominably stupid of me. That's one area where I truly have changed. Having gone through so much unhappiness with Eleanor, and feeling like I'd besmirched the family name with a failed marriage, I wanted to make certain the world saw that I hadn't made a second mistake. I worried far too much about appearances, which isn't even who I really am. I'd never worried about such things before. My mother *did* influence me. I'm not trying to throw the book at her. I should have been adult enough not to let that happen. I so wanted to make her proud of me. She still saw me as a boy, and I was used to letting her make major decisions about etiquette. I love my mother, but she does come from a different generation. It was up to me to bring her round to more modern thinking. I hate to admit it, but the five years we've been apart, while heart-wrenching for me, have also been good. They gave me time to figure out what my beliefs are, as opposed to my mother's."

"All of this sounds wonderful, Kit, but how am I to know that these feelings are legitimate? If I were to return to our marriage, how do I know you wouldn't revert back to your old ways?"

"I suppose you can't know that with certainty without giving it a go. If it develops that I'm not telling the truth, or even lying to myself, there's still the possibility of divorce. Shouldn't we at least see if we can put this thing back together again?"

Kit turned toward Lily. There was no question in her mind that if he truly felt the way he said he did, she wanted to be his wife again. Perhaps it was time to find out if he'd relinquished his strange ideas about making love. Lily knew, beyond any shadow of a doubt, that no matter how much she loved him, she would have to refuse to spend the rest of her life in such an odd arrangement. She was a warm, passionate woman, and she wanted more from her husband. She couldn't go back to pretending.

He kissed her, sweetly at first, and tentatively. Then his arms tightened about her, and she returned his passion. The kisses grew longer and deeper. Kit pulled away and stood up. He reached for her hand and said "Come, Lily. Let's go to your room. We're still husband and wife. There's nothing wrong with sharing our love."

When it was over and Lily had returned to earth, she lay snuggled in her husband's arms, emitting a small giggle.

"What is it Lily? Why are you laughing?" Kit asked.

"I was only wondering, after such a performance, if you still believe that women who enjoy making love aren't ladies?" she answered.

"You are the most exquisite lady I've ever known. What a fool I was to waste even one precious moment of our intimate time with priggish, Victorian beliefs. I loved my father dearly, but that was the worst piece of advice any father has ever given a son," Kit laughed.

Lily snuggled down further onto his chest. "Oh Kit, we've both learned so much. This is only the last hurdle. I think we have a much clearer idea about what marriage entails. I realize now that it can be quite simple. If both partners love the other with equal fervor and take the time to show it with affection and communication, there's no reason the marriage can't be grand."

"I heartily agree, Lily. I intend to spend every day for the rest of our lives showing you how dear you are to me. I so admire your strength and courage, your independence and desire to be the best you can be. I'm sorry I ever said the things I did about your wish to become a physician. That's another foolish notion I picked up from my parents. I've watched you struggle and dedicate yourself to what is surely a calling, and I'm so proud of you I could burst."

"That means the world to me, Kit. Because it's true that medicine seems to be a part of me. While the last years have been very difficult at times, I've adored every moment of my training. Now I'm terribly anxious to go out into the real world and practice what I've learned."

"Will you return to Claybourne Court when you graduate? Please, Lily. I'll make it as easy for you as possible. I want you there, by my side, helping me to grow, too. I realize your passion for medicine, and I'm delighted that John is so hopeful that you'll become his partner. I won't interfere with those plans in any way. I have my own life, running the estate, and making certain that the new woolen mill operates smoothly. But, I do look forward to our sharing a home again, and you being there for Win during these last years before he leaves for boarding school."

"Yes, Kit. I want those things too. I don't think there's any question that I'll return to our home, and we'll begin a new, better life together."

There was silence while he kissed her again. "Kit, what of your mother? Will there be any difficulty where she's concerned?" Lily asked.

"No, Lily. She's very much aware of the changes I've undergone, and while we don't always see eye to eye, she's begun to understand that I'm my own man. Frankly, I believe she'd like to see you return to Claybourne Court. She's getting older and would rather spend her days away from the challenge of being the woman who presides over such a large estate. Do you think you'd be up to a good, long talk with her, sharing many of the things you've told me about your love of medicine and how you'd like to see our marriage progress?"

"I'll be happy to speak with her, Kit. I have to tell you just one thing, though. Lady Cynthia needs to understand that I'm not the shy, unworldly little girl who once worked at Claybourne Court. Of course she's owed great respect as your mother, but I want her to recognize that I expect equal respect as your wife."

"That's fine, Lily. I believe she's ready to hear that. Secretly, I can see that she's extremely proud of what you've accomplished. I've overheard her singing your praises to various people."

Lily laughed. "Well, that's a surprise to me, but a nice one. I think we can mend the fences, and with forgiveness we can grow to be close once again."

Kit spent what was left of the night with his wife. When they woke the next day, no one looked askance as they emerged from the same room. A fool could tell from the looks on their faces that the past evening had been a watershed moment.

2

On June 22, 1925, she heard the words she'd longed to hear for as long as she could remember. "Doctor Lily Claybourne," called the Dean, as each graduate accepted her diploma with enormous pride.

When the graduation ceremony reached completion, Lily joined her loved ones in the auditorium. After cuddles, kisses, and words of congratulations, they all went outside where a large tent had been set up as a reception area. Refreshments were being served, and people were mingling about. New graduates were unrolling their diplomas and reading the coveted words upon them. Everyone was asking Lily what her plans were, now that she was a full-fledged physician.

"I won't be such until I sit for my examination, which will allow me to be registered. But, I feel quite certain that I'll do well on those. After that, well... I think all of you may be surprised at what I have to tell you."

Everyone stopped talking and waited for Lily to continue. Of course John and Gena wouldn't be surprised, nor would Kit, but the rest would be knocked-for-six.

"Is everyone ready for a big surprise?" Lily asked.

Everyone nodded their heads and murmured.

"Get on with it Lily," John smiled.

"I have wonderful news, and I've purposely waited until after I had my diploma in hand before I told everyone. I'm four months pregnant, and by November Kit and I will have a new baby in the nursery. So, I'm coming back to Claybourne-on-Colne and going into practice with John Garrett. I'll be handling all of the obstetrics and gynecology patients, as well as pediatrics. John and I have discussed this at length, and the legal work has already been completed."

Lily knew that Kit was delighted. He'd been totally astounded when she'd presented him with the news about her pregnancy, but in a happy way. Pia and Win both seemed thrilled. Win said that he would love to have another brother, and Pia said it didn't matter what gender the baby was, she just wanted Lily to be well and the baby to be healthy. Both kissed her. Lily didn't care whether they had a girl or a boy. After all, Kit had his heir to Claybourne Court, so it didn't matter from that standpoint.

Her family and friends all crowded round, and Lily accepted their good wishes. Then, they mingled a little with the other graduates, who were all exchanging compliments with one another on their success. Finally Lily felt they could leave. Kit had the car waiting outside with Edward at the wheel, ready to drive them back to their London home. Since it couldn't accommodate everyone, only the immediate family crawled into the Rolls, and they drove off back to the house. The future looked very bright indeed, and Lily couldn't remember if she'd ever felt so complete. She was a medical doctor, with a family she loved, a husband she adored and a new baby on the way. She could never have asked for more.

When they arrived at Claybourne-on-Colne, Lily took herself off to John Garrett's surgery immediately. John was surprised to see her on her first day at home, but he couldn't have been more pleased. He and Gena had only returned themselves a few hours before. They sat down and discussed how their office arrangement would work, and it was clear that there was no reason why it shouldn't run smoothly. There was plenty of room in the cottage for two physicians, and they worked out who would be situated where. John's practice had flourished, and he had more patients than he could handle. He felt that adding Lily as his partner would ease his load tremendously and offer the village a marvelous alternative, since women generally adored female doctors who had expertise in their special branch of medicine. Lily would begin her practice with a ready-made patient file.

She wandered through the cottage, where she had once lived with her parents, when her father was the physician in Claybourne-on-Colne., Lily chose her childhood bedroom as the place to be reincarnated as a nursery. It was large enough for a sitting alcove for Emma, the nanny, and Lily could scamper upstairs to see the baby in between appointments. She knew Kit would agree to such an arrangement. Emma should probably have been long gone, but Kit had kept her on since Win adored her, and she'd been there when Kit had traveled to London on weekends. Win didn't always accompany his father, making it necessary for someone to be on the premises to look after him. He wasn't by any means old enough to be left alone without adult supervision. Mrs. Briggs and the others on staff at Claybourne Court couldn't be taken away from their responsibilities to monitor Win. The new scheme would entail Lily taking the baby and Emma with her to the surgery during working hours. That way, Lily would always be close by. John was perfectly satisfied with the arrangement.

Win was still spending a month in the summertime with his American grandparents. They came to England to be with him. Usually for a week or two after that, he tended to be sassy, and hard to deal with. They learned to stay away from the subject of Eleanor. The Evanses had filled his head so full of untrue stories about her, and naturally he wanted to believe them. He seemed to have forgotten all about the terrible way she'd pinched him continually, and the time she'd kicked him in the ribs and called him a "brat". Those memories had been replaced with a lot of silly nonsense about what a sweet and kind mother she'd been, and how often she had played with him and given him cuddles. Neither Kit nor Lily had any desire to hurt their son's feelings by producing a letter they had kept that Eleanor had written to Win. It contained overwhelming proof that Eleanor was a wicked, evil person. Thus, for the present time, they allowed him to unwind from his annual visits with the Evanses, and then slowly return to the loving boy they'd always adored.

Jordan Thomas Claybourne was born on September 10, 1925. It was a routine delivery and Lily did beautifully. She worked until one week before the due date and felt marvelous until her first labor pain. Jordan was a beautiful baby, with Kit's blue-green eyes, and Lily's auburn hair. Win was thrilled about having a brother, and everyone at Claybourne Court adored him. Lily stayed home for the first six weeks and then returned to the medical practice with John. She had passed her exams in July and was registered. She had full hospital privileges at the new hospital, and even though it was named after Kit's family, she didn't expect any special treatment. Her patients adored her and Lily took a lot of time and attention with them. It took Kit time to acclimate to his wife working as a physician, especially when she had a tiny newborn to watch over, but he *did* adapt, and slowly realized that the scheme she'd worked out was functioning beautifully. Kit and Lily were the happiest they'd ever been and couldn't see a reason in the world why that wouldn't continue. Christmases and summers came and went, with galas, agricultural fairs, the growth of Lily and John's medical practice, and Win's entrance to Eton, in the autumn of 1928.

Leaving Win at school was a heartbreaking moment. Kit and Lily made every attempt not to let him to see their anguish, but it was hard. What made it even more difficult was the fact that Win suddenly didn't want his parents to go, which surprised them. Win had always been an independent child, sailing to America with his nanny, and riding his pony, Bean, for miles and miles when just a little boy. Yet it was apparent that he was going to be abysmally homesick, and they hadn't even left yet. It wasn't a good beginning. Kit knew from his own days at boarding school, that the older boys were likely to bully Win for what they would consider baby-like behavior. There was a conversation with the Headmaster, who assured them Win would adapt quickly. He advised that they say their goodbyes, and be on their way without lingering. Kit and Lily accepted his advice, and told Win that it was time for them to leave if they were to make it back to Claybourne Court before mealtime. Win's lower lip trembled, but he valiantly tried to keep from falling apart completely. Lily hugged him with all of her strength, and Kit put his arm about his shoulders.

"Now then, Son, we'll be on our way. Remember Mummy and Daddy love you very much. Have a jolly time, but follow the rules. We know you'll make many new friends very quickly. I'll write to you a lot. Study hard and before you know it, Christmas will be here and you'll be coming home again. We'll be anxious to hear all about your adventures," Kit said.

"I don't want to stay here," Win replied, as a giant tear rolled down his cheek. "I hate it here. I don't think the other chaps are friendly."

"But you don't know them yet, Win. You must give them a chance. If you're friendly to them, I think they'll be friendly to you."

"No. I can tell. They're going to be mean. I want to go home with you. I want to go home to Bean."

"You're getting too large for Bean, sweetheart. We were thinking about giving Bean to Jordan, and then getting you a brand new horse. When you come home your new horse will be waiting for you."

Win began to cry harder. It had been the wrong thing to say.

"Nobody is ever going to take Bean away from me. I don't care if I'm too big for her. Bean is strong. A lot stronger than she looks."

"All right," Lily answered. "We can discuss this when you're home. Let's not worry about that now."

"If you leave me here, I'll run away," Win threatened.

Kit and Lily exchanged a concerned glance. "Now Son, that wouldn't be the done thing. You know how much that would worry us. We don't want to think of you being unhappy."

"Then take me home with you," he repeated.

"We can't do that, Win. You're going to be just fine. Now, Mummy and I are going to leave. I think you'll be better after we've gone. The Headmaster will take special care of you."

Lily reached down and cuddled him, ending with a big kiss. So did Kit. Then, before Win could answer, they turned and walked away. Lily was furiously dabbing her eyes with a lace handkerchief. Edward was parked across from the school's chapel, and they slid into the back seat. "Hurry Edward, before Win runs over and begs you to take him home with us. He's most upset and doesn't want to stay."

"Poor lad," replied Edward, as he turned the car around. "Going off to board can be ghastly."

"Will he be all right, Kit?" Lily asked, in between sobs.

"Yes. I believe so. We'll check on him. This isn't uncommon. He'll adjust."

◦◦◦

They didn't say a lot to one another on the drive back to Claybourne Court. Lily wept off and on during most of the trip. It was awfully good to arrive home. She immediately went to the nursery and held three year old Jordan tightly. She wanted to pick up the telephone and ring the school, but in her heart she knew it wouldn't be wise. After playing with Jordan for a bit, she went to her own room for a lie-down. Kit went outside to speak with Henson about issues concerning the estate.

When night fell, the house seemed empty and Lily hoped that Win wasn't sobbing into his pillow. Kit came to her and they held one another. "This is the most difficult part of being parents, Lily. Having to let them go. It's the best thing for him, but he doesn't understand that yet."

"Were you all undone when you went away to board?" she asked.

"Not that I recall. But I wasn't inclined toward homesickness, and I'd had a more stable home life."

"Yes, I can see where that would have an effect," Lily replied. "Poor Win. It's been one thing and another. His upset makes me feel guilty for ever having left to go to London."

Kit reached over and held her hand. "Nonsense. Win knew that you still loved him dearly. He knew he could see you whenever he wished, or ring you up. No, it wasn't ideal for him, but he was in school himself. Don't blame yourself, Lily. Millions of children experience homesickness. You, my dear, are the pediatrician."

Lily gave him a watery smile. "All of that goes out the window when it's your own child."

As they sat in the drawing room, wondering what their son was going through at that moment, the telephone rang. Mrs. Briggs answered and called Kit to the hall phone. Kit picked up the receiver.

"Lord Claybourne. This is the Headmaster at your son's school. I'm calling regarding Winford."

"Yes," answered Kit. "What about him? Is he all right?"

"Well, we aren't certain," the voice replied.

"I beg your pardon? What do you mean you aren't certain?"

"He seems to have disappeared."

"What the bloody hell do you mean, he's disappeared?"

Lily heard his raised voice, and the language was totally uncharacteristic of Kit. She quickly made her way into the great hall. Standing next to him, she tried to understand what had happened.

"Lord Claybourne, as you probably know, he was most upset when you left. I believed he would settle down when we all went into the dining hall. Unfortunately, he didn't. As I'm sure you're aware, boys of this age can be somewhat nasty. Because he was obviously upset, continuing to weep, a group of the older chaps began to tease him. It developed into a food fight. Many of the boys were disciplined and sent to their rooms. I kept Winford behind and brought him to my office."

"Win," shouted Kit. "Win. That's his name. That's what he's called. If the other boys heard 'Winford' that probably added to the commotion."

"Quite possibly, Milord. But I feel rather certain that it was his continued crying and carrying on."

"All right. So, what happened next?"

"I left him in my office for a few moments. I had to carry on with settling the group of ruffians. One of the older monitors passed by my office and noticed that your son was on the telephone. I hadn't given permission to use it, but I thought perhaps he'd rung you. Did you by any chance hear from him?"

"No. Not at all. Do you know who he rang?"

"I contacted the trunk operator and was told that the call was made to Windermere."

"Windermere? Oh my God. His grandparents are in Windermere. He spent a month with them in August. But the school is much too far for them to have picked him up. Have you initiated a search?"

"Yes, we did. He isn't anywhere to be seen. Let me ask you. Did the boy have any funds on him?"

"Yes, of course. He had the amount the school recommends for a term. He was supposed to turn it in to the office, where I understood it would be doled out weekly. Did he not do so?"

"No, I'm afraid not, Lord Claybourne. So, would he have had a goodly sum – enough for instance to have bought a train ticket to Windermere, or somewhere else that the grandparents might have instructed him to meet them?"

"Yes. Certainly. More than enough. Have you checked the train schedules?"

"Yes. No one remembers seeing a boy of his age. But, as you can imagine, there was quite a crowd on the trains returning to various locales, since so many parents were leaving their boys. Of course there would have been other children, too, since many families brought siblings along."

"So, in other words, he could be anywhere," Kit said, raising his voice. "Anywhere."

Lily started to weep. It was perfectly apparent that Win was missing.

Win boarded the train to London. He wasn't in the least frightened, since he'd taken the train many times from Claybourne-on-Colne to London while Lily was in medical school. Chad and Dorothy Evans told him to meet them under the clock at Victoria Station. They were leaving at once in their chauffeur-driven limousine. He would reach London before they arrived, but he was told to stay there and that they would come for him. By the time they finally met up, it was nearing midnight. Dorothy Evans found her grandson curled up in an uncomfortable chair. She rushed to him and took him into her arms.

"There now, precious baby. Tell us everything that's happened. Pappy and I are here, and you're safe."

Win was so glad to see them. He'd known if he rang them, they would come. He also knew he was in trouble with his parents. He wanted to leave the station before they came looking for him. "MeMe can I tell you in the car? I'm awfully tired. Can we just go?"

"Of course we can," she answered. Taking him by the hand, they made their way out of the station to the waiting car. Win glanced about self-consciously. He was too old for someone to be holding his hand like a baby. Chad Evans told the driver to take them to Claridge's Hotel where he'd reserved rooms. After they were settled in their suite, Win told his version of the tale.

"My parents don't want me anymore, now that they have my sister Pia and my new brother Jordan. They decided to send me away to board. I didn't want to go, but they made me. When we got there, they told me they were going to give my pony, Bean, to Jordan. You know how much I love Bean. Well, I started to cry, and a bunch of older boys were mean to me. They said they were going to push my head in the loo. We were all made to go into dinner, and the same boys started throwing food at me. I was covered with gooey stuff. The boys were sent to their rooms and I knew what would happen if I went to my own room. I had a chance to use the phone and decided to ring you because I knew you'd help me. I want to go to America with you. I'll bet my real Mummy would never have sent me away to school."

"Of course she wouldn't have. And, of course we'll take you home with us. Pappy is going to get us reservations on the first ship to New York," answered Dorothy.

"Will I have to go away to school over there?" Win asked.

"You'll have to go to school because it's the law, but you don't have to sleep away from home. Pappy and I will find a good school where you can go during the daytime. I'll write to your parents after we're at sea. They should know where you are. But, Pappy and I intend to tell them that we're going to the court to seek custody of you. From what you've told us, they don't deserve to have you."

Win felt a lump in his throat. He knew he'd told lies, and that his parents would be hurt. Well, they weren't exactly lies. He'd just left quite a few things out of the story. He would miss them if he went to live in America, but if he stayed in England they'd make him go back to the school. Anything was better than that. Besides, he knew that his parents hated his real Mummy, and he was sick and tired of never being able to talk about her. It was their own fault. They shouldn't have sent him away. So he pushed aside the guilt feelings and started to think about his upcoming trip to America.

Kit and Lily were greatly upset. They were certain that Win was with his grandparents, but had no idea where. They had the number for the house the Evanses leased every summer, and they rang it immediately. There was no answer. They could be anywhere. The most likely scenario was that they'd collected Win and were planning to return to America with him. Kit and Lily didn't have the faintest idea where to look. Knowing Win was with his grandparents eased their anxiety a bit, but it was beyond the pale that Chad and Dorothy Evans would do such a thing. They had to know that Kit and Lily would be beside themselves with worry. The idea that they might take him to America without his parents' permission was akin to kidnapping as far as they were concerned. They considered calling Scotland Yard, but were hesitant to bring the police into the matter. If the Evanses were returning to America by ship, it would still be enormously difficult to check the many ships departing England en route to America. And who knew what route they were taking? It was possible that they were going by way of Spain, France, or any number of route combinations that would eventually land them in the States.

Surely Chad and Dorothy weren't so cold-hearted that they wouldn't contact Lily and Kit telling them of their plans. But one never knew. They'd always harbored resentment over Eleanor's death, and it wasn't hard to see that they'd never believed Kit when he'd told them what a horrible mother Eleanor had been. Trying to understand the Evans' motives was doing no good, and by the time morning broke, Kit had decided he *would* contact the authorities. It seemed to take forever to get through to someone who could understand the entire tale and had the authority to make decisions. The police said they would begin with a list of hotels in London to see if an older couple accompanied by a small boy had registered, and then would proceed to check rosters of ships leaving any port in England.

In the meantime, the Evanses, accompanied by Win, checked out of Claridge's. Chad had made reservations on the S.S. *Californian*, leaving Southampton late on the morning of September 28, 1928. They had a car and driver, so didn't have to deal with public transportation. By the time Scotland Yard had the case, it was already too late. It didn't take a long time to reach Southampton from London, about an hour and twenty minutes. As soon as they arrived, the ship was ready for boarding and they were in their staterooms in a matter of minutes. They had booked two adjoining rooms.

Chad paced. He knew Kit Claybourne wasn't likely to sit around and do nothing. He would feel infinitely better when the ship got underway. Win's primary concern was that he didn't have any clothing, besides what he was wearing. His grandparents reassured him that they would outfit him from head to toe. At long last there came the sound of the ship's horn, and the giant liner began to move. Before they could settle down, there was a safety drill on the top deck. After that, they returned to their cabins and rested before lunch. Both Chad and Dorothy were vastly relieved when they reached open sea. In seven days they would be back in Virginia, and Chad would be speaking with his attorney about the chance of suing for custody of their grandson.

3

When the S.S. *Californian* had been at sea for two days, Kit and Lily received a wire. It wasn't specific. All it said was: '**AT SEA. WIN WELL. BEGGED TO BE TAKEN TO VIRGINIA. LETTER TO FOLLOW. CHAD EVANS.**' Not a word about what ship they were on and no information about when they would arrive, presumably, in New York. Obviously they weren't about to have the ship stopped and the child removed.

Kit was as irate as Lily had ever seen him. He paced, ranted and raved until the Evans' letter arrived. When it did, two days later, he became even angrier. He felt helpless. It was written by Chad, and didn't even begin with the usual niceties.

Lord Claybourne;

We're sorry to have disturbed you in this manner. However, Win seemed desperate to be with us, and we felt the best thing would be to take him to Virginia. We were fearful that he might otherwise do something drastic. He was bordering on irrationality. He wouldn't consider returning to Claybourne Court. He told us that he did not want to go away to boarding school at all, but that you made him do so. In our opinion, no child should ever be forced to leave his home. He was very upset about the prospect of having to give up his pony, Bean. I have promised to take care of any expenses involved in transporting Bean to Virginia.

Win has had a difficult childhood. His head has been filled with things about his mother that are untrue. He doesn't understand why anyone would say nasty things about a woman he loved dearly. I might add that she loved him just as much. It seems that some sort of scheme has been at hand to cause Win to have a wholly false image of his mother. It's difficult for us, Eleanor's parents, to know that she is being maligned to her only child. Now, to learn that you have gone so far as to tell him that he isn't wanted, and that you are taking away one of the few things that brings him joy, is beyond comprehension. Adding two more children to the family has only served to make Win feel as though he has never been enough for you, and especially for Lily. Add to that, Lily having left him at an exceedingly young age to move to London and resume her studies. In our opinion, that was akin to abandonment. When Lily's training was finally over, instead of returning to care for her son, she immediately went to work and showed very clearly that her primary concern was the new baby, Jordan. It was Jordan who was taken to work with her daily, while Win was left to fend for himself. In my wildest imagination, I cannot imagine our Eleanor doing such a thing. At any rate, we feel very strongly that Win will be a happier, more loved child with us. What could be nicer than growing up where his mother became such a charming girl? He will feel close to his roots and will heal from the neglect. Rest assured, Win's education won't be ignored. We will find an excellent day school for him, but he will not have to worry about being told he isn't wanted anymore. I think it only fair to tell you that I already have an appointment to meet with a fine attorney in New York City before we return to Cloverhill. I intend to sue for custody of Win, which I'm sorry I didn't do long ago. Win does love you, and I know in time he'll write to you about his own feelings. I'm sorry it's come to this, but cannot say that I'm totally surprised. I'm thankful that we were in England when this nightmare unfolded, or God knows what might have become of him. I hope you'll try to see this situation in its true reality. I have no doubt that you love Win, in your stiff upper-lipped, aristocratic, British way, but he needs much more than that. The kindest thing you can do for him is to allow him to do what he wants. That, of course, is to live in Virginia with us. You're welcome to see him in Virginia at any time,

although I must say I believe it would be better to let him acclimate to his new surroundings without causing any more pain or confusion.
Chad Evans

"This is the most incredible bunch of drivel I have ever read in my life. Can Win really have said these things about us?" shouted Kit. "He knows very well we didn't send him to school because we didn't want him anymore. Why would he lie about these things?"

"Oh Kit, who knows why children do things? He was totally beside himself with worry the moment of our arrival at the school. Looking back, we probably should have brought him home and tried again in a year. He couldn't have gone back to the Beaudesert Park School because they don't take them past thirteen, but I'm certain I could have found someplace else. I took the cue from the Headmaster, who has surely gone through this sort of thing countless times. He seemed to have it well in hand. We should have listened more closely when Win threatened to run away."

"Lily, we aren't going to start blaming ourselves for this. He's obviously told some lies here. At no time has anyone said that he was unwanted. And he has conveniently left out the part about getting a new horse, more appropriate to his size. There was never any intention to rid ourselves of Bean. He knows that."

"Kit, he must have felt frantic. He said what he thought he needed to say to touch their hearts. Just think if the situation were reversed. If we heard that sort of tale, we would rush to the child's defense, too. The question now is what to do about it?"

"Obviously the first thing I need to do is get in touch with an excellent barrister who specializes in this sort of case. I suppose we'll need an attorney in America. Isn't that what they call barristers there? God, I hate putting Win through this. Unless we can convince him to tell the truth, it could become very messy."

"Kit, we still have the letter we found where Eleanor tells Win all of the things she did, such as pinching, and kicking him. I hate to show it to him, but I do think it would go a long way in proving that if this is the sort of person that Chad and Dorothy Evans raised, what sort of parents would they make for Win?"

"Yes. Where is that letter? In the safe?" Kit asked.

"Yes. Shall I get it? It's been so long, I scarcely recall everything in it."

"Do you think it will hold weight in an American court?"

"I would hope so. We'll need to be able to prove its Eleanor's handwriting," Lily replied.

"I don't see a problem there. I still have letters Eleanor wrote when I was in France. They would serve as a perfect vehicle for comparison."

"Isn't it possible that a smart barrister, or attorney, or whatever they're called, will try to claim that she wrote those things in a moment of depression and that the emotions in the letter don't reflect her true personality?"

"Anything is possible. Let me get the letter. I'll be back in a tick." Kit hurried up the staircase to his bedroom, which held the safe in its wall. Dialing the combination, he found the missive lying neatly on top of a pile of papers. He remembered the day he'd come upon it. It had fallen from an Emily Post *Book of Etiquette* in the library. Obviously, Eleanor had worked on it for some time. He closed the safe, and brought the letter back down to Lily. As she re-read it, she noticed something peculiar for the first time.

"Kit, have you noticed this before? I believe this letter was written at two different times. She begins talking about how she isn't a 'baby' person and the like. Remember, this was when she was leaving for London, after you came home from France with your injured eye. But further on, she makes reference to things that took place much later, like the times she pinched him and when she dropped him at the Christmas gala, kicking him, and calling him a 'brat.' She must have begun the first part when she planned on moving to London, but for some reason never posted it. So she slipped it between the pages of the book and there it stayed until she apparently went back to it when she returned to Claybourne Court, after the London house was bombed. When she started to write more, she makes reference to the episodes that took place on Christmas Eve. I wonder when she had time to do that? Perhaps she grabbed it when you told her to get out and took it to her room to complete. That was such a confusing time. I thought she went straight outside, but she may not have. I'm sure she knew she was in deep trouble. She wanted Win to know her side of the story. I remember the Australian soldier saying that they went directly to the gazebo. That may be true, but perhaps when he left she sneaked back and retrieved the letter. She'd definitely put it back where she kept it hidden in the library, because it wasn't with her when she was killed."

"Lily, I'm sorry but I don't see what difference this makes?" Kit said.

"Perhaps none. But if a good legal expert tries to argue that the actions she describes are completely out of character for Eleanor that can quite easily be refuted by proving that the letter was written at two different times."

Kit reached over and kissed his wife. "Lily, you would have been as fine a barrister as you are a doctor," he smiled, adding the first bit of levity to what had been a dreadful evening. "I see what you mean now. Let's put it back in the safe, but we must remember to take it with us when we speak with our barrister."

The S.S. *Californian* docked in New York harbor just as the timetable indicated. Dorothy gathered up belongings, making certain that she had Win's passport. Thank god it had been with him. The school had given instructions that all students have a valid passport since, during the school year, trips were often scheduled to places like Ireland and even Paris. Dorothy had bought several items of clothing for him on board ship, and planned to do more shopping in New York. Once they disembarked, they checked into the St. Regis Hotel and she unpacked. Chad grabbed a taxi and headed to his attorney's office in lower Manhattan. Dorothy took Win to Brooks Brothers and outfitted him with a new American wardrobe. Then they all met back at the hotel for afternoon tea. Chad was encouraged by what he'd been told. Basically, Win would have to carry the day. His testimony was crucial. In essence, they were trying to prove that Kit and Lily were unfit parents, and the story that Win had told backed up that assertion. The attorney, Mr. Roger Brewer, said that he wanted to speak to Win before they left New York. An appointment was scheduled for the following day. The case would not be a trial, as such. It would be a meeting in the judge's chambers with each party and their legal representatives. Then Win would have to speak with the judge, in private, under oath.

Both of his grandparents went with him to speak to the attorney, and Win performed quite well. And it was, indeed, a performance. He told the same story he'd told his grandparents when he'd met them in London, embellishing it here and there with more elaborate details about how Lily had taken Pia with her when she moved to London to attend medical school, but didn't care about Win's feelings. Win said that he'd felt much unloved and just "in the way". He explained how the nanny had been kept on, even though he was too old for such care. He said he saw very little of his mother during those years. Of course he didn't add that Lily had asked him if he wanted to move to London, and that he'd flatly refused. His intentions weren't precisely malicious, but he was enjoying the attention, and everyone was treating him like such an important grown-up. He didn't have much understanding concerning the consequences of his actions. A date to meet with the judge was scheduled six months in advance. With the legal arrangements having been made, the Evanses and Win boarded a train for Virginia.

The next thing Kit knew, he received a letter from Mr. Brewer saying that he and Lady Claybourne would have their depositions taken in three months at the New York offices, of Brewer, Brewer and Porter. Kit was furious and called his own barrister for advice. He was told that it would be best if the Claybournes retained their own American attorney, and he gave them the name of a gentleman he felt was excellent. His name was Randall Crawford. Kit wrote to Mr. Crawford at once and received a trunk call from the attorney shortly thereafter. After listening to the entire story, he advised Kit and Lily that it would be wise for them to comply with the request for a deposition, because otherwise the likelihood of a subpoena was great, and that wouldn't look good to the court. Lily and Kit made plans to travel to America, but they were stunned that it had taken such a frightening turn. They wished they'd had the opportunity to speak with Win alone before then, but were further advised not to make an attempt to do so until the deposition was over. There was too much likelihood that they might be charged with attempting to interfere with Win's testimony.

On March 14, 1929 Lily and Kit boarded the *Mauretania*, one of the finest ships of her time. She was a Cunard line passenger ship, known as the "grand old lady of the sea". Neither of the Claybournes was happy about having to make the trip. Letters between lawyers were exchanged for months, and Kit was in perpetual shock. How had it come to such horror? There had been no communication whatsoever between parents and son, although Chad did write an occasional letter giving Kit and Lily minimal information.

When their ship harbored in Manhattan, Lily and Kit immediately took a taxi to the Waldorf Astoria Hotel. They had no idea how long they would be in New York, so simply made an open-ended booking. They absolutely dreaded the scheduled deposition the following morning and wondered if Win would be present.

When they arrived at the attorney's offices, Win was not there. Kit and Lily were relieved. Lily knew she would have broken down and wept if she'd seen him. It seemed unreal that the boy she had loved from the day he was born had chosen to put them through such agony. She kept trying to remember that he was only thirteen years old and had probably got himself in over his head in his panic to leave school. But it had become a very serious matter, and the rest of his young years now depended upon how the suit turned out.

The entire day was spent in the attorney's conference room, where question after question was put to both of them. Lily was not allowed to listen to Kit's answers, nor was Kit present when Lily was interrogated. They weren't particularly nervous, as they knew that they were telling the truth, but on the other hand there was the grave concern that the entire picture could be misconstrued. Women in America, especially in the upper classes, seldom worked outside of the home, any more than they did in England. One issue that loomed large was the fact that Lily was a physician and cared as much for her medical practice as she did for responsibilities in the home. Of course, that wasn't really true, but persons in the legal profession were very good at twisting facts to match the point they were trying to make. After both depositions were finished, Lily and Kit sat down with the attorney who explained to them how the case would proceed. In just over a week they would meet with the judge, as would the Evanses. Following that, Win would also be questioned by the judge. The judge would make the final determination about who would have custody of Win. Win's testimony would play an enormous part. Since he was nearly fourteen years old, his preference would be given a lot of weight. Essentially, if he was adamant in his wish to stay in Virginia with the Evanses, the judge would likely grant them custody.

Ten days later, they were all present in a New York City courtroom. It was the first time Lily and Kit had seen Win since the sad day they had left him at the boarding school. They were surprised to see how much he had grown and filled out.

The Evanses were called into the judge's chambers first and were gone for approximately an hour. Win sat on one side of the courtroom, and Lily and Kit sat on the other. Not a word was spoken. Lily dabbed at her eyes with a handkerchief, but made no attempt to communicate with Win. He sat reading the book *Black Beauty* and didn't raise his head. Finally the Evanses returned and the Claybournes were asked to take their place with the judge. When they entered the chambers, the judge stood and welcomed them. They all shook hands. Then they were both sworn in. The judge's name was The Honorable Eric Jensen, and he seemed like a nice person. He asked them many questions about their marriage, and the home they provided for Win. Kit and Lily were completely honest. They especially made the point about how dearly they loved their son, and explained that in their opinion the entire situation had become out of control. It was truly their belief that Win had rung his grandparents in a panic, never dreaming it would end up in a legal battle. When they were finished the judge thanked them and they were dismissed. Win would be the next person to be summoned.

That would be the moment of truth. Would Win be honest? When he sat down in the big leather chair, facing the judge's large desk, it was explained to him that although they weren't in a courtroom, the principle was the same. He was under oath and was required to answer each question truthfully. The attorneys and Judge Jensen explained to him what "perjury" meant and he looked ashen. He was picking at his fingernails and fidgeting.

"All right," Judge Jensen began. "I want you to tell us in your own words exactly how this all came about."

"I didn't want to stay at boarding school," Win answered.

"So, because you didn't want to stay at boarding school, you phoned your grandparents. Is that right?"

"Yes. I knew they would come and get me."

"Why didn't you want to go back to your home?"

"Because I knew my parents would just make me go back to school, and I hated it."

"Why did you hate it?"

"Because there were mean boys who called me names and threatened to throw me in the loo."

"Did you tell your parents that you didn't want to go to boarding school before they enrolled you?"

"Well, no, not exactly. I didn't say much one way or the other. I just knew it wouldn't do any good. That's where my dad went to school, and I was supposed to go there, too."

"Why did your parents say that you had to go away to school?"

"Because they didn't want me anymore."

"Young man, did they actually say those words to you?"

"Well, they sort of did. They didn't have to say anything, I just knew. My step-mother had another baby, and between that and her medical work, she didn't care about me anymore."

"So, you just knew in your heart that your step-mother didn't love you?"

"Yes. That's right. She tried to pretend, but then both she and my dad would make mean comments about my real Mummy. They didn't want me to love her, even though she's dead. I would never have known about how sweet and nice she was, and how much she loved me, if it hadn't been for my grandparents."

"And because of that, you've now decided that you would rather live with your grandparents in America?"

"Yes, because I owe that to my real Mummy. Daddy didn't like my Mummy anymore, but he fell in love with Lily. Daddy got rid of Mummy, so he could marry Lily."

"What do you mean 'got rid of her'?"

"Well, he didn't really do it. But, she was so unhappy, she ended up getting murdered. If he'd still loved her, she wouldn't have been where the murderer could find her."

Unbeknownst to Win, Judge Jensen had the letter that Eleanor had written, so he was very familiar with the facts. "All right. Tell me about your home. Does it have a name?"

"Yes, sir. It's called Claybourne Court. It's very old. Someday I'll be the one to take care of it, when I'm the earl."

"Won't that be hard to do, when you're living in America?"

"I guess I'll have to go back to England then."

"Don't you think you will need some training before you take on such a large responsibility?"

"Well yes, I guess. My father is supposed to teach me the things I need to know."

"How can he do that if you don't live there?"

"I'm not really sure."

"Win, where did you go to school before your parents sent you to board?"

"I went to Beaudesert Park School. I loved it there."

"How far did you have to walk to get to your old school?" the judge asked.

"Oh, I didn't walk, sir. It was about fifteen miles away. Edward, our chauffeur, took me and then collected me at the end of the day."

"Hmmm. With such cruel parents, who didn't want you, I should think they would have made you walk."

"They still wanted me then."

"I see. It was only when it was time for you to go to board that they decided they didn't want you anymore?"

"Yes, sir, I guess.

"How many other children did you share a room with at your home?"

"Not any. It was my own room."

"How many people shared the bathroom?"

"I had my own private loo, sir."

"And your own pony?"

"Yes, but my parents said they were giving her to Jordan, my little brother."

"Did they say you could no longer have a pony or a horse?"

"Um, well, yes they said I could have a new horse, but I didn't want a new horse, I wanted Bean. She's been my pony forever."

"Win, are you happier with your grandparents than you were with your Daddy and step-mother?"

"Well, I was happy lots of times at home. I just wasn't happy away at school."

"Are you happier with your grandparents?"

"I love them. They're very nice to me, and I think I would hurt their feelings if I said I didn't want to stay with them. After all, they came all the way to London to meet me, and didn't make me go back to that awful school."

"Do you think you're hurting your parents' feelings by saying you don't want to live with them anymore?"

"I guess. I saw my Mummy crying outside in the other room."

"Why would she do that if she wants to get rid of you?"

"I don't know. I guess she feels bad."

"Win, I want you to think about only your feelings. Don't make a decision based on anybody else's feelings. Now, tell me the honest truth. Who would you rather live with? Your parents or your grandparents?"

There was quite a lengthy silence. Win fidgeted around some more, and bit down on his lip. He put his head down and didn't meet the judge's eye. Finally, he spoke. "Well, I guess I'd rather live with my parents, if I didn't have to go away and live at school. But, if I have to live at school, then I'd rather be with my grandparents."

"So, in other words, Win, if I were to convince your parents that perhaps you aren't quite ready to go to a school that requires you to board, you'd be perfectly happy to go home with them."

Win began to cry. "Yes, sir. I miss them a lot. And I miss my pony, Bean, and my brother, too."

"All right. I think that settles what we need to know. I'll speak with your parents and your grandparents. I believe this can be worked out satisfactorily. You can be excused now. Thank you for being honest with me, Win."

And so, after passenger ship expenses, attorney fees, non-refundable tuition, and tremendous anxiety, Win came home. The Evanses were shown the letter Eleanor had written so many years before, and while it shocked and hurt them, they agreed that their daughter had not been a proper mother. They came to an understanding with Kit and Lily that Eleanor would no longer be spoken about in glowing terms. The four of them also reached an agreement that Win was old enough to make up his mind regarding trips to

Virginia. Everyone shook hands. Lily had a sneaking hunch that the Evanses had discovered that caring for a thirteen year-old boy was not all roses and sunshine.

4

Life settled down at Claybourne Court, and Lily went back to her medical surgery, while Kit was working harder than ever to keep a keen eye on production figures at the new mill. He'd hired an excellent man to head the company, and the operation was running smoothly. Kit borrowed a considerable sum of money to start the operation, but he anticipated paying it back within five years. At that point, the business plan projected that the loan would be paid, and the mill would be showing a profit. Thus far, the figures confirmed that they were on track to meet the goal.

Win was home, where he belonged, wishing he'd never left. The entire fiasco had left him with feelings of guilt, and he had a greater understanding about the reasons for not acting too impulsively. He knew that if he'd called his parents instead of his grandparents on that awful day, things would have been very different. It was a situation that got completely out of control. Kit and Lily didn't punish him for his behavior, as it was obvious he was punishing himself. He promised that he would never tell another lie and apologized for hurting them. Kit and Lily understood from the start how it had come to pass and, between themselves, they spoke of the Evans' actions. If they had only rung Kit and Lily instead of sweeping Win up and carrying him off to America, the entire mess could have been averted. No matter. It was done and over. Win stayed out of school for the remainder of the year, but Lily did assign him a list of over fifty books that he had to read before the following school year began.

He didn't like leaving home much anymore, but in time that fear faded. He still loved to ride Bean, and there was no more discussion about giving the pony to Jordan. Win would know when he was ready for that. Even when he went riding, he didn't stray as far from home as he once had. Lady Cynthia, who hadn't known anything of the frightening ordeal until after it was over, kept an even keener eye on him than she had. She and Lily had their long overdue chat and both came away from it committed to a better and closer relationship.

Pia was coming to the end of her years at Chateau Mont Choisi. It had been a wonderful experience, and she had matured enormously. Kit and Lily were planning to attend her graduation in May and promised to take Win with them.

Jordan was nearly four years old and Lily doted on him completely. He still made trips back and forth to the medical office with her, but as he grew Lily often brought him with her in the morning and then made certain to have him back in the nursery by the time Kit returned to Claybourne Court in the afternoon.

The promise of a trip to see Pia in Switzerland had a wonderful effect upon Win. He loved Pia so much and hadn't seen her since the previous summer, so that was a great part of his excitement. But the idea of a trip to see a foreign country was also exhilarating. The question of whether Win would go away to board at school loomed large. It had to be discussed, yet Kit and Lily dreaded even mentioning the subject. They got advice from numerous people, and still had no idea how to approach the dilemma. Some said to let him broach the subject; others said he should be made to return and to apologize to the Headmaster; still others said that he should be allowed to remain at home with a governess. None of those choices were appealing to Kit and Lily. Finally they decided to have a look at another excellent school with a wonderful reputation in Northwest London. There was no significant difference between the two, except of course to those who attended one or the other, for they were fierce rivals. Kit and Lily thought that a fresh start might be the best thing. There was no question that Win would have been embarrassed to return to a place where he'd had such difficulty. At least some of the boys who had bullied him would undoubtedly still be there. Thus, on a sunny day in April, Edward drove them to see the second school. Win was very quiet during the ride, and Kit and Lily kept up the chatter. Upon arrival, they simply strolled the lovely grounds, stopping to watch a cricket game. When they came upon the school stables, Win's face brightened.

"I didn't know they had riding here," he commented.

"Yes, in fact a boy is allowed to take his own horse, if he so desires," Kit answered.

"You mean I could take Bean?"

"Yes, although I suspect most of the chaps your age would have horses, not ponies. Of course, that's up to you. If you were to decide you wanted a bit larger horse, we could arrange that, but if you want to keep Bean, that's fine too." Kit chose his words very carefully.

"Well, Bean might be afraid to go away from home. I think it might be better if I let her stay at Claybourne Court and maybe got a new horse."

Kit breathed a sigh of relief.

"Win, my primary concern is whether you think you're ready to go away from home. You weren't very happy before. Your father and I can search about for other schools where you could attend during the daytime and come home at night, like you did at Beaudesert."

"Well, Mummy. You see, after going to America and being away for such a long time, I think maybe I wouldn't be so unhappy. I like this school better."

"Why is that, Son?" Kit asked.

"Because the chaps look friendlier."

Of course there was absolutely no difference in the appearance of the students at the two schools, but Kit and Lily weren't about to argue.

"Would you like us to make an appointment to meet with the Headmaster?"

"Umm – let me think about it for a few days," Win answered.

They drove back to Claybourne Court with a glimmer of hope, but Lily continued to search other schools, just in case. Within a few days Win announced that he would like to meet the Headmaster and to go away again.

In May Lily arranged her schedule so she could come home a little earlier in the day. She wanted time to enjoy the outdoors with Jordan. Kit accompanied them, meandering over the green lawns of the estate. Lily pushed Jordan in his pram, and Win trotted alongside riding Bean. The trees were veiled in misty green, and daffodils were blooming in a thick carpet of gold. As Lily strolled across the lawns, she couldn't help being overcome with memories of the years she'd been at Claybourne Court, and by everything that had happened during the time since she'd married Kit. It had been 1914 when she'd first found her way to what was now her lovely home. There had been so much turmoil, so much stress and unhappiness, but amazingly she and Kit had persevered. Now she had a seven month old miracle in the pram and a lovely thirteen-year-old boy beside them. She was anxious to have Pia back where she belonged, too. Of course Pia's plan was to go on to school in Paris, but Lily harbored a small hope that perhaps she might have had her fill of being away from England. Some of her more recent letters indicated a longing to be home with family. But, Lily also knew that she had to be realistic. Pia was twenty-three years old now, and would want more out of life than being buried in the country. It would be wonderful if she decided to settle in London, but all her parents could do was wait and see what their daughter's thoughts were when they saw her at the end of the month.

The day finally arrived and their luggage was placed into the Rolls Royce. Upon departure, Lily hugged little Jordan tightly and smothered him in kisses. She hated leaving the little tot. It would be her first time away from him, and while she looked forward to the trip, she despised leaving her tiny son. Thank God they had Emma, who was a true treasure. They would be gone just over two weeks, and Lily knew it would seem like a lifetime. She double and triple checked the list she'd made up for Emma, which the nanny didn't really need, since she knew the routine as well as Lily.

After several more kisses, they said last minute goodbyes to everyone else in the household, as well as to Lady Cynthia, and Edward drove them to the station. They would be boarding a train for London and then on to Dover, where they would take the cross-channel ferry to Calais, in France. It would be the first time that either Lily or Kit had returned to France since those awful days during the Great War. After they arrived in Calais, they would board another train that would take them through Paris and on to Lausanne, Switzerland.

When they boarded the cross-channel ferry in Dover, Kit made certain to point out the White Cliffs of Dover to Win. Both parents told him about how their hearts had swelled with love for their homeland when they'd seen those splendid white cliffs upon returning from battle-ravaged France. Those cliffs had become an iconic symbol to all who'd longed for the green valleys and sheep-filled meadows in their beloved England. Win stared at them wide-eyed and said he would always remember how his parents had felt as their ships passed that emotional landmark.

Then, on the train from Calais to Paris, Kit pointed out various other landmarks to Win. He explained about where he'd been stationed during the war, and how there had been a hospital at Calais which was where he'd been cared for by John Garrett, whom Win called Uncle John. Lily explained to him where Aubigny was, too. It was amazing to both Lily and Kit that the scars of the war had healed in what seemed a short period of time. In reality, it had been less than ten years since the war ended, but France seemed to be thriving, and small villages were back to being sleepy havens tucked into the countryside. However, they weren't traveling through the areas where some of the worst fighting took place. Had they been, they would have seen that there were still stark reminders of horrific battles. It took more than a decade to replace trees that had stood for generations, and for ground that had been scorched by the devastation of war to return to meadowland once again.

When they arrived in Paris, they had a very short layover until boarding the train to Lausanne and heading off toward the French Alps. They had a sumptuous dinner in the dining car and slept in berths designed for overnight travelers. Win thought it was the most incredible adventure he'd ever had and begged for an upper berth. He said that sleeping on a train was a lot more fun than sleeping on an ocean liner.

When they woke they were not far from their destination. There was still snow at the higher elevations, and Win began to talk about the prospect of skiing. After Pia's graduation they had plans to stay for three days at the Victoria Jungfrau Hotel in Interlaken where they would have views of the famous Jungfrau Alps. As the train descended into valleys, the ground became green and lush. They passed charming homes, with sod roofs and flower boxes spilling geraniums. Cows dotted the lovely landscape. It was an enchanting land. Everything looked so pristine, and as they chugged on through small villages, rosy-cheeked Swiss men and women, waved at their windows.

Finally they came into Lausanne. Kit had been there before when he'd brought Pia to visit the school, but it was all new to Lily. Beautiful Lake Léman was a glorious blue in the streaming sunlight, but because it was still early in the morning, there was mist across the water. They gathered up their belongings and readied themselves for disembarkation. As they stepped from the train, their lovely daughter stood on the platform, eagerly awaiting their arrival. Pia looked stunning. She had changed during the short time that had passed since they'd last seen her. She was taller and, if possible, even more willowy. Lily rushed to her, embracing her with great love. Win was practically jumping up and down, waiting his turn. He absolutely worshipped the ground she walked on. Pia squeezed him with all of her might and told him how horribly worried she had been about his ordeal in America.

"Yes, but Pia, it all worked out. I made it home," he replied.

"I know that, Win. Father told me all about it in a letter. I'm so very proud of you for deciding to come back. How courageous you were."

"Yes. Well, it wasn't very hard to decide. I shouldn't have called my grandparents. It was rather dumb of me, actually. But Mummy and Daddy feel that I learned a valuable lesson."

"Yes, little brother, I think so. I'm just awfully glad it worked out so well," Pia smiled.

"Can we go skiing while we're here, Pia?" Win asked.

"Oh no, Win. Not at this time of year. There isn't enough snow."

"You mean there's no snow in Switzerland? That doesn't seem right," Win declared. "I thought there was snow all of the time."

"Well, there is, very high up in the Alps, but that isn't a place for a young boy to be skiing. Especially one who has never skied before. But it's very beautiful, and you'll love it, I promise."

"Okay," Win murmured, with some disappointment in his voice.

Kit put his arm around his daughter and kissed her on the cheek. "You look beautiful, as usual. I'm so happy we can all be together for your special day."

"Well, Father, not quite all. Little Jordan isn't here. The last time I saw him was at Christmas. He was so small. Who does he most resemble? You or Lily?"

"He's a very handsome chap, so I would say he most resembles Lily," Kit laughed.

"Oh Kit, don't be so modest," Lily replied. "He has your eyes and your smile. I think he'll be a copy when he grows, lucky chap."

The four of them continued down the platform where Kit found a porter to take their bags, and then hailed a taxi cab. He had booked rooms at the historic Beau-Rivage Palace Hotel, opened in the 1800s. The driver deposited them at the front entrance, and they were in their rooms in a matter of minutes. Pia's graduation ceremony was to be held the next day, so that night they were free to enjoy an excellent dinner in the superb hotel dining room.

Following dinner Pia took a taxi back to her school, and plans were made to meet after the ceremony which was to take place at exactly noon the following day. Lily, Kit and Win rose early, had breakfast in their suite and dressed for Pia's graduation. By twelve o'clock they were seated in the front row with all of the other families who had come to see their daughters and sisters leave Chateau Mont Choisi. The ceremony was held out of doors, on the shores of Lake Léman. It was a splendid day and the Claybournes were filled with immense pride as they watched beautiful Pia gracefully walk across the stage to accept her certificate. Lily's eyes filled with tears when everyone stood as the band played Pomp and Circumstance. Her heart burst with pride for the sixteen-year-old girl who had arrived at her door on a windy, cold morning.

Interlaken and the Victoria Jungfrau Hotel changed their lives. Of course it was magnificent, which everyone had expected. But what had not been expected was that a convention of the top cinema producers and directors in the world was being held at the hotel. The first night, when they attended dinner in the dining room, heads turned as Pia walked to the reserved Claybourne table. At five feet eight inches tall and weighing under eight stone, with flawless skin and perfect features, she made a stunning impression. In a matter of minutes several people, both men and women, came over to where she was seated and presented business cards, asking if Pia was represented by anyone. They all assumed that she had already been signed by a studio and was an actress. It was clear from the beginning that God had placed Pia in the right place at the right moment. They were all there; D.W. Griffith, Carl Laemmle, Samuel Goldwyn, William Fox, Adolph Zukor, Louis B. Mayer, Harry, Albert, Samuel and Jack Warner, Alfred Hitchcock, Fritz Land, and Jean Renoir. Pia was breathless at the attention she was drawing, and her parents weren't certain how to react. Pia had dreamed of an acting career as far back as Lily's time in medical school, while living in London. Lily had never discouraged it, but she believed the chance of such a thing was quite remote. Not that Pia wasn't lovely enough. She rivaled any of the known actresses of the day, but the possibility of being discovered was something Lily thought unlikely. The film industry had flourished in England for a period of time in its very early days, but the Americans seemingly had a lock on the fledgling industry. They'd produced the first "talkie", The Jazz Singer, in 1927, and if one wanted to become what was being called a *star*, one had to go to California. Now they were sitting in a posh hotel dining room in Switzerland, practically surrounded by the biggest names in what was fast becoming a superlative industry. Win was wide-eyed as well. He was a very keen fan of American western films.

Pia looked at her father with an expression that mixed excitement and wonder with fright. Kit decided he'd better take things in hand. When the next individual approached their table, he stood and offered his hand, saying that his daughter appreciated the attention, but that her family wished to enjoy a quiet dinner together. Then he signaled the maître d' and asked for assistance in being allowed privacy. The Claybournes were immediately escorted to a private dining room, where they could enjoy their meal in peace. Pia looked relieved, but also a bit downcast. Kit took time to reassure her that she hadn't seen the last of the cinema moguls.

He was correct. When they exited through the main dining area, a queue of men, and one woman, Alice Guy-Blyche, had formed, waiting to introduce themselves to the exquisite Pia. She was dressed in a simple frock in her signature white linen, sleeveless, and chemise in style. At her neck, she wore the pearls that Lily had given her so long ago when she'd first arrived at Claybourne Court. Her hair was styled in a bob, with a pixie-like fringe that brought even more attention to her magnificent, dark eyes. Her years at Chateau Mont Choisi had added to her natural grace and poise, and while she was secretly terrified of so much attention, she didn't allow those feelings to show. Kit kept his arm round her waist, and Lily stayed close by her side. Win smoothed his hair down, looking expectantly at the horde of people, hoping they might notice him as well. Kit stepped in front of the masses of people. In an authoritative, but friendly voice, he introduced himself to all and said that he was going to reserve a separate room in the hotel where Pia could make appointments to speak with people individually. He would arrange for half-hour appointments, and if anyone wished to make one, they could ring the front desk. Pia was astounded, as she'd heard nothing of the plan. That was because Kit hadn't formed it until a moment before. It seemed the only plausible way for Pia to speak with those who were showing an interest in her. The Claybournes continued on to their suite of rooms, and when they arrived, Kit rang the desk. He explained their needs and was assured that they would be assigned a room where interviews could take place, and the hotel would set aside one of their clerical staff to take care of making appointments. Pia was beside herself with excitement. She'd never even attended drama school, but it looked like she might be able to sign with a major studio.

After a full day of speaking with people she'd only dreamed of meeting, Pia was terribly confused. The best offers came from American film studios, yet she had a fear of going across the pond to California by herself. She hadn't given anyone an answer at the end of the very long day. Instead, she spoke at length with her parents while dining in their room. The only British company that offered a contract was British International Pictures, a studio with which Alfred Hitchcock was affiliated. They were planning on releasing their first talkie picture the next year. After a long conversation with Kit and Lily, Pia decided to sign with them, since it meant staying in England. At a later point she thought perhaps she might go to America after she'd experienced working for an English studio. It was the culmination of a dream, and when she signed on the dotted line, Pia's heart soared. She was going to be a bona fide actress.

5

Pia Claybourne's introduction to the world of film was well planned and well executed. It wasn't long before her name was on the lips of people from all points of the globe. Her photo could be found in newspapers from the United States to Australia, and from Tokyo to Rome. Rome was, indeed, probably the city most enamored with Pia. Her life story was a made-for-cinema drama. It had all begun in Rome, and thus, the city claimed her as their own. Pia didn't fabricate or enhance any of the details about her birth, nor about the romance between her mother and father. In fact, what had been a foolish lark for a young college boy, became a heartwarming romance. Kit, who once would have been mortified by such publicity, now smiled wryly and shook his head. Lily was thrilled that Pia was receiving such worldwide acclaim. Win carried a picture of her with him at all times, showing it to his mates at school every chance he got. Lady Cynthia, of course, was a different story. Having long ago given up on the reputation of the Claybourne family, she reiterated her feelings that this was what she had feared all along. Kit simply patted her on the back, telling her that the modern world loved such a tale, and that the entire family should be thrilled for Pia. Funnily enough, when photographers came to do a story on Pia and her family, it was Lady Cynthia who arranged the sitting and gave instructions about what each person was to wear. She also insisted upon being photographed standing next to her granddaughter with a look of great pride on her face.

By the end of the year, Pia was the featured actress in a film that eerily mirrored her life, about a young girl who grew up in poor circumstances and then discovered that she was the daughter of a titled Englishman. The family didn't see her often as she was totally under the thumb of the British International Pictures studio in Borehamwood, Hertfordshire. Occasionally she would dash home for an unannounced weekend, but primarily she lived in a small flat in that quaint English town, which was fast becoming known as the "Hollywood" of England.

As time passed, Claybourne Court returned to a semblance of normalcy, with the addition of photos of Pia prominently displayed. Kit's woolen mill was up and running, and thus far, he was pleased with what the figures were showing. Lily continued with her medical practice and it flourished as the small village of Claybourne-on-Colne began to grow in population. She and John had gained an outstanding reputation as top drawer physicians, and because Lily was the only female obstetrics and gynecologist for hundreds of miles in any direction, she had so many patients that she had to extend her hours. Jordan continued to make his trips to her office with Emma, and Kit said that the little boy wouldn't even need an education. He would just take up a scalpel someday and start practicing. He was growing into a fetching child, with darker hair than Win had at his age, more on the order of Lily's. His eyes were a duplicate of Kit's, with their blue-green color, and he definitely had his father's mouth and face shape. Since Win was at school, Jordan had all of the love and attention that had once been showered upon his big brother. He was an exceptionally good little chap, and Lily even said she would sign on for another baby if she could be assured that the temperament would be as sweet as Jordan's. It looked like everyone in the Claybourne family had settled into a comfortable lifestyle, and although sometimes things seemed a bit hectic, the routine was well established. Pia would be home for Christmas, as would Win, and the family was looking forward to one of the rare times when they would all be together. Pia's film had been released to rave reviews, and everyone was excited to hear about the new life she was living. The Christmas gala would be held, as usual, and the family suspected there would be a full house, since Pia would be an added draw.

But, in October, one of the worst crises in history hit Wall Street, in the United States. The newspapers were filled with stories of what was being called "Black Tuesday", October 29, 1929, when stocks plummeted and panic reigned. Masses of people tried to sell their stocks, but no one was buying, and yet, the stock market crash was only the beginning. Since many banks had invested large portions of their client's savings in the stock market, the banks were forced to close when the markets crashed. This caused another panic across the nation. People rushed to the banks to withdraw their money. The massive withdrawal of cash caused additional banks to close, and those who hadn't made it to the bank in time were bankrupt. Like dominoes falling, manufacturers began to cut back on workers, and unemployment rose to astonishing levels. Kit followed the news with increasing concern. A great deal of his money was invested in the United States stock market. Suddenly it was gone. He said nothing to Lily about his growing panic, but it was clear that such a dreadful calamity would have a monumental effect on the entire world, including England. He had taken a large loan to implement his woolen manufacturing plans, and there was grave doubt as to whether he would be able to pay it back.

When Christmas came, everything went on as planned. The gala was an enormous success, and as predicted, Pia was definitely the shining star. If possible she looked even lovelier than ever, dressed in a white silk gown with long sleeves and a high neck. Pia's sense of style had always been one of her greatest attributes, and it seemed to develop even more as she matured. Her taste was always very simple. She was living proof of the old adage that "less is more". She had learned from Lily how to present herself as elegant and chic. No one present that night would have guessed that there was the slightest ripple of unrest in the Claybourne family. Kit was his refined, genteel self, and Win, who had grown to be nearly as tall as his father, sent many of the young girls' hearts racing. Lily kept Jordan near her side all night. He had just turned four years old in September. Win was potty over him, and scarcely moved without making certain that Jordan was with him. Similarly, Jordan idolized his older brother. It showed in the way he gazed at Win with awe.

There was a lot of talk among the men about the stock market crash in the U.S., but most were quoting the well-known and highly regarded economist John Maynard Keynes who had said, upon learning of the stock market crash, "There will be no serious direct consequences in London. We find the look ahead decidedly encouraging." Kit was holding tightly to those words, although he had already suffered dearly, due to his investment in American stocks. As soon as the holidays were behind him he intended to sit down with his bankers in London and take a hard look at the reality of his own financial situation.

After the gala ended, Pia called her family into the drawing room and announced that she had signed a contract with a well-known studio in the United States. She would be leaving for California at the beginning of the New Year. The American studio had bought out her contract from British International Pictures for a princely sum, and Pia had tripled her income. She was absolutely glowing with excitement and pride, and it would have been difficult for her parents to voice any negative views. Kit and Lily were happy for her good fortune, knowing that career-wise it was definitely the best move she could make. The only thing they were pessimistic about was the fact that she would be going so far away from home. But Pia was a grown woman, and they'd always known she was special. Now the entire world was finding that out. Not only was Pia an incredibly beautiful woman, but she definitely had true acting ability for which she credited her Italian temperament.

The New Year arrived, and with it came Kit's talk with his London advisors. The news was devastating. He had lost all of the capital he'd invested in American stocks, and the outlook for manufacturing looked extremely grim. At least a twenty-five percent drop in the export of manufactured goods was expected, which would include wool from the Claybourne Mill. The prediction was that most employers would begin to cut wages, which meant there would be less buying power. He was advised to close the mill and declare bankruptcy. In addition, there was serious doubt as to whether Claybourne Court could be kept afloat. He left the banker's offices feeling immensely depressed. Upon arrival back at Claybourne Court he'd reached a decision. Except for the servants, the house was quiet. Lily was at the office, and Emma was there, too, along with Jordan. Of course, Win was off at school for his second term. Kit went to the safe in his library and retrieved the revolver he'd been issued during the war. He checked that it was fully loaded and, leaving the house, he walked briskly, filled with purpose, toward the stables. Eden greeted him, and Kit asked that 'Spark O Fire' be saddled and readied for a ride. Once on the stallion's back, he trotted in the direction of the woods.

Lily returned to Claybourne Court shortly before the noon hour, ready to lunch with Kit and to allow Emma time for her own mid-day meal, while Jordan had his lie-down. She was perplexed to find that Kit was absent. She began searching the house. When she came to the library, she saw the safe ajar, and Kit's life insurance policy lying in plain sight on the top of the desk. There was an empty box of ammunition next to it.

Lily threw her hand to her mouth and gasped. There was no question in her mind about what Kit planned. She began to run as fast as she could, out of the house, toward the stables.

"Yes," Eden answered, when she questioned him about her husband. "'E went for a ride on Spark O Fire".

Lily didn't even wait for Taffeta to be saddled. As the mare was led out of her stall, Lily leaped atop her back. With skirts flying, she galloped to the woods. Kit hadn't expected that she would return home until much later. Generally they didn't have their mid-day meal until closer to one o'clock. He'd not traveled a long way on the trails. He'd calculated the approximate distance that the sound of a gunshot would travel, since it was important to him that Eden hear the report and discover his body. He never dreamed that Lily would arrive first. He was sitting on the ground in a copse of trees, while his horse grazed on some tender clover. The gun was resting in his lap. Upon hearing the sound of another horse, Kit quickly turned his head, startled. His eyes widened when he saw his wife.

Trying to remain calm, Lily said in a firm voice, "Kit, whatever the problem is, that is not the answer."

He lowered his head and began to sob. Lily dismounted and approached him. "Oh Kit. What can possibly have brought you to such despair?"

He raised his head and looked at her, pain etched on his ashen face. "Lily, we've lost it all. It's gone. All of our money. We're ruined. I've spoken to the bankers in London. I was supposed to be a steward of this magnificent property. My father trusted me to continue the legacy. My insurance money will cover the mill loan and the taxes on Claybourne Court. It will allow you to continue your lifestyle. I can't bear being the first Claybourne to fail."

"Kit, you aren't thinking straight. What you're saying is foolish. You once said you wanted us to be partners in life, to be a team. That's what we are. Not just in good times, but now, when everything looks bleak. You have me. You can lean on me. You've carried this burden alone, and you don't need to any longer. Together we'll find a solution."

"Lily, there is no solution. The money's gone. How will we live?"

"We'll live by using our brains. There are all sorts of things we can do, starting with selling the London house. Even in a depressed market, it's a lovely home and it will fetch a nice amount. I'll sell my jewelry, we'll move to the Dower House and close up Claybourne Court until after the slump. We'll call the servants together and explain our dilemma. Many are near or past the age when they may wish to take their pension, or go to live with their own families. We'll have a meeting with the tenant farmers. They'll be told that they may cut their tithes in half in return for providing us with foodstuffs. My salary is quite good, Kit. It will pay for taxes and our daily living expenses. I know that Will and my mum will be glad to pay Win's school expenses, and Pia just signed that wonderful new contract. I'm sure she would be happy to help. We'll do whatever needs to be done." Lily put her arms round her husband and kissed him lovingly. "Kit, it's time to find out what we're made of. I love you, and I know you love me. Together we can get through this, and we'll be stronger for it. Now come. Give me that foolish gun, and let's have no more talk of insurance policies. Let 'Spark O Fire' take you back to the stables, and let's go up to the house. We have a lot of thinking to do."

6

Time moves slowly sometimes, very slowly. That was true of the period known as the Great Slump in England, or The Great Depression in America. Lily's strength was beyond comprehension. Kit wrapped his pride around him like a cloak, but sometimes it seemed too much to bear, and he nearly broke. Then he would sink into another deep depression. Lily's strength brought him back up and pulled him through. Britain's world trade fell by half, and the output of heavy industry fell by a third. Profits plunged in nearly all sectors. In the summer of 1932 unemployment was at three-and-a-half million, and many more had only part-time jobs. The industrial and mining areas of northern England, Northern Ireland, and Wales saw unemployment numbers hit over seventy percent. The income tax rate was raised to twenty-five percent. Many Brits said that the country had never recovered from the depression brought about from the Great War, which had begun in 1914. There was, undoubtedly, much truth to that statement. Some portions of the economy did better than others, particularly when it came to the manufacture of items like automobiles, electrical appliances, and other new inventions. But Kit's mill, which produced wool from which sweaters, blankets and other products that England had always been known for, didn't offer any new commodity.

The first thing Lily and Kit did was to call all of the staff together. They were extremely honest with them and said frankly that they were facing ruin. They asked each to think carefully about their options. If they chose to stay at Claybourne Court, it would be at reduced wages. They would not be staying in the Great House, but instead would move to the Dower House. Thus, accommodations for live-in staff would be severely restricted. There were small cottages on the estate that had been built years earlier to accommodate servants who were too old to carry on with duties. They were meant to be used as housing for staff who received a pension, and allowed them to live out their years on the estate they had served so faithfully. Lily told those of the staff who had been with the Claybournes the longest, that they could accept one of the cottages and that a small pension would be paid. Only two servants chose that route. Mary, the cook, wished to stay on, but said that if she could make her home in one of the cottages, she wouldn't accept a pension, but would work for reduced wages. She was granted her wish. Halsey also wanted to stay, but as a retired pensioner. Actually, that worked out rather well, because Lady Cynthia had a butler at the Dower House. Michael Richmond, Kit's valet, had family in Cornwall and said that he would rather go to them. He told Kit and Lily that he had been saving his wages for many years and wouldn't need or accept a pension. Both of the footmen had family in Wales, and they chose to go to Penbryn and Cardiff to help them. They too had savings put aside. The parlor maids chose to return to their parents. They hadn't been with the Claybourne family for long and were still young, so no pension was due them. Of course Emma stayed on to care for Jordan. Lily promised that she would make every effort to pay her full wages. Edward, the chauffeur, also chose to stay. He had been with the family for over twenty years and was already settled in the carriage house. He said that he could survive on half-pay until the nightmare ended. Everyone else left except for Mrs. Briggs, who had cared for Kit when he was a baby, and Eden, who wouldn't have been able to sleep if he didn't have the stable.

The next item on the agenda was calling together the tenant farmers. Kit explained the morass they'd found themselves facing, and all stood around in a circle, kicking the ground, and looking like it was just one more disappointment in their pathetic lives. However, Lily and Kit presented them with a plan that brought smiles to their faces. They were told that instead of their tithes going to the Claybourne family, the money would be set aside so that they would be purchasing the land they farmed. In time they would own their own property. If they weren't able to pay every month, they needn't fear eviction. In return, they were asked to donate a quarter of each crop to the Great House, and to assist with putting up canned goods. Henson had approved the scheme, and Kit was grateful for his input. Not one tenant farmer left.

Lily sat down and looked at the financial statement for the surgery. It was very encouraging. The practice was thriving, and her portion of the profits was substantial. She decided to increase her hours, while still allowing one day a week for people who couldn't afford medical care. She worked until eight o'clock each night, all day Saturday and a half day Sunday. It was a grueling load, but the extra money would go a long way toward meeting the payroll at the mill, paying off the loan and providing living expenses.

As Lily had hoped, her mother and Will immediately jumped in, picking up expenses for Win at school, as well as Jordan at Beaudesert. It was Jordan's first school year, and Lily was so grateful that he would be able to follow in his brother's footsteps. In addition, Pia sent half of her salary. Last, but certainly not least, Lady Cynthia, who had a rather large stash from her inheritance when the old earl had passed away, pledged to contribute everything she had to see that Claybourne Court lived to see better days. She didn't argue with the suggestion that the entire family move to the Dower House and immediately set about making up beds and arranging rooms to accommodate everyone satisfactorily.

It was a monumental undertaking. In addition to all of the changes at Claybourne Court, the London townhouse was also put on the market. Kit and Lily were fully aware that it was a bad time for the sale of property, but the house was paid for, and anything they could get for it would help them survive the dreadful depression. As it turned out, the house sold almost at once to a wealthy American who had not put all of his money into the market and was buying up property all over the globe. He also showed interest in whether or not Kit would be willing to sell any of the land that made up the acreage at Claybourne Court. After much deliberation, the decision was made to sell 1000 acres, which didn't please Kit, but the money garnered put them on solid footing.

After all of the changes, it was a matter of holding rigidly to the budget they'd drawn up and praying that the economy would improve sooner rather than later. But as the 1930s moved along, everything became worse instead of better. Unemployment continued to rise. Although the Dower House was substantially smaller, everyone made it into a cozy home, and there were no complaints. Later, when they reflected on that time, it was amazing that it was seen as one of the most tranquil periods of their lives. Certainly there was a loosening of restraints with no fancy dinners and no Christmas galas. Meals became much less opulent, and entertainment consisted of songfests around the piano or parlor games. There was croquet on the lawn in the summer, as well as simple picnics. The tenant farmers were invited to participate, and they did join in. Knowing that they were going to be owners of property on the estate caused them to feel more like they belonged, and one could almost see their self-esteem rise.

When Win came home during the summers, he and Susie Gatewood still rode horses together. They pitched in to help with fertilizing and weeding crops. Susie became very good at putting up canned goods with the rest of the ladies in the kitchen. While the ostentatious lifestyle they had enjoyed was gone, the sense of pulling together to accomplish a goal was very fulfilling. In 1933, Win turned eighteen years old and moved on to Oxford. By then Kit had managed to put aside enough money so that, when added to what his grandparents were so generously providing, Win's costs at the famed university were covered. During the entire period, Win didn't hear a word from his American grandparents. Everyone assumed that they too had been hit hard by the Depression. Win wrote to them on several occasions, but they didn't reply. Perhaps they were frightened that the Claybournes would ask for their help, or maybe they didn't want to admit to their own devastating situation. Most people in Claybourne-on-Colne seemed to fare decently. John and Gena were all right, due to John's thriving practice and Gena's decision to lend a hand, thus saving the expense of a nurse in the office. All of Gena's children were in school, so she was able to give time to John, Lily, and their patients. Will and David Morris escaped financial ruin by being in the right profession. No matter what the economy, people still got sick, and still needed remedies and elixirs. Thus, a chemist's shop was a relatively stable business. They were extremely generous with their customers who had difficulty paying their bills, although those seemed to be few and far between. Over all, Claybourne-on-Colne was a self-sufficient little village made up of middle class families, and other than the Claybourne Mill, there was no manufacturing. Naturally agriculture had been hit hard, but the village wasn't comprised of a great many farms. Many of the inhabitants were retired people who had moved to the quaint Cotswold village after a lifetime of working in London or other larger cities throughout England.

After Win's first year at Oxford, in 1934, he asked Susie Gatewood to marry him. It was the first bit of truly happy news there'd been at Claybourne Court since 1929. Even Lady Cynthia, who once would have been apoplectic at the thought of her grandson marrying the daughter of a tenant farmer, was pleased as punch. She'd grown very fond of Susie over the years. Susie was the sort of girl everyone adored. With her dark, tousled curls and big blue eyes, she was an adorable young lady. They had moved from being playmates as young as five years, to being breathlessly in love at eighteen. Susie had graduated from *The King's School* in Gloucester and had plans to go on to study nursing at the same college Lily had attended, *The London School of Medicine for Women*. While nursing too had once been considered "not acceptable", since the war it had become an honored profession. Win was well aware that his family had a long history of serving their nation in the military, and after Oxford he planned to enlist in the British infantry. Kit was surprised at that news, since Win's love of airplanes had given everyone to believe that if he entered the military he would be interested in the Flying Corps, or the Royal Air Force. Win and Susie didn't plan on marrying until after both had finished their education, but they wanted it clearly understood that neither one of them was available to anybody else. Because money wasn't easy to come by, Lady Cynthia gave Win her engagement ring to present to Susie. It was a lovely sapphire surrounded by small diamonds, and Susie couldn't believe her eyes. Who would have believed that Lady Cynthia would willingly see the ring she'd been given by the last Earl of Gloucester slipped on the finger of Susie Gatewood? Time had a way of healing old wounds. A small party was held at the Dower House for the happy twosome, with Karen Gatewood unable to take her eyes from her precious daughter. She had loved Win like a son for years, and it seemed he was already a member of the family. Win kept his arm round Susie's waist during the entire celebration. Mary splurged and made a lovely cake, and Kit even dug into the wine cellars in the Great House and found a good aged vintage to serve for the special occasion.

Undoubtedly the absolute worst year of the Great Slump was 1934. The world's economy hit rock bottom. As the situation seemed hopeless, more and more people began to turn to whomever promised them a better life. The rising leaders used people's fears and prejudices to rally support and create a scapegoat for the world's problems. In Germany the country turned to Nazi extremism with the election of Adolph Hitler in 1933. By 1934 he had declared himself Führer, or absolute leader of his country. But at that time, what was occurring in Germany was still not prominent in the minds of the British people. Little did they know what an impact Adolph Hitler's grandiose dreams would have on them in just a few years.

However, there was no event in the world that took priority over that which occurred on August 13, 1934, at Claybourne Court. It carried the power to wipe out all thoughts of the economic slump, German re-armament, and rumors of the Prince of Wales' love affair with a twice divorced American woman.

Lily left for the office early, after enjoying a quick breakfast with her husband. His spirits had risen enormously since the beginning of the family's financial difficulties, and his pride in Lily was boundless. He had slowly but surely begun to take control again, and was seeing success at the Claybourne Mill. Because the entire family had pulled together, it appeared that they were going to survive the frightening events of the last half decade. The country wasn't out of the woods yet, but the Claybournes were holding their own and felt good about what they had accomplished. He kissed his wife goodbye, telling her he loved her, while she replied that he was the light of her life. They smiled, and Lily raced off to see patients. Win was still home from Oxford, but was already off with Susie for the day. They were busy riding horses and making wedding plans, although the day was still far in the future. Jordan, now nine years old, had finally inherited Bean, and he was in the riding ring while Eden taught him the correct maneuvers for jumping. Pia was home for a visit, trying to make up her mind whether to remain in the United States or return to England, which was starting to establish a robust film industry. She had made such an incredible name for herself that she could virtually write her own ticket, and she still loved her adopted English homeland, not to mention her family. She sat with her father at the table after Lily left for the surgery.

"It's so pleasant to have you here, Pia," Kit spoke, leaning back in his chair and patting his mid-section. "Goodness, Pia, I believe I ate too much. I have a bit of indigestion. Do you think I should call Lily and ask her if there is something I should take for it?"

"Is it different than other times you've had it?" Pia asked.

"Not necessarily. Perhaps a bit more niggling. I'll not bother Lily. She'll think I'm becoming a hypochondriac," he laughed. "Anyway, just looking at your lovely face is enough to make me feel splendid."

"Oh Father, it's so very nice to be home with you and Lily, as well as Win and Jordan. Isn't it amazing to think of the changes since I first came to you? Here's Win at Oxford and announcing his engagement, while Jordan is growing like a weed. It's been such a difficult time for the family, but I'm so proud of how we all banded together and did what had to be done to save our home."

"The credit for that in large part goes to Lily. When the crash came, I was completely useless to anyone. If it hadn't been for Lily, her marvelous organizational skills and straight thinking, I don't know what might have happened."

"But, whatever *might* have happened, it didn't, Father. I know Lily was wonderful through all of it. But you were smart enough to know when to let her make some of the decisions. If it hadn't been a joint effort, it could have torn the family apart. Many families didn't survive this crisis, both here and abroad. California has been overrun with pitiful people who've been hit not only by the Great Depression, but by the terrible dustbowl that ruined the land in the Plains States. I'm really growing a bit weary of California. It is a lovely place in many ways, but it's changed a good deal since my arrival and, at heart, I'm an English girl, I'm afraid."

"Are you ever going to marry and think about giving us some grandchildren, dear Pia?" Kit asked teasingly.

"Oh Father. I'd very much like to have a husband, home and family, but I haven't time to meet anyone. Either I'm filming a movie, or studying the script for another. I truly have no social life at all. The studio decides who I will or won't see socially. It's all rather factory-like."

"Come home to us, Pia. That would mean the world to us, especially to me. We'd see you so much more often, and there are British lads by the dozen who would like to take you home with them. You've paid your dues. It seems to me that you can make your own decisions now, with no harm to your career."

"Yes, I think you're probably right. That's the way I've been thinking, too. When I listen to some of the speeches made by government officials, I begin to worry that there are faint rumblings of war beginning in Europe. I don't want such a thing to happen and not be here in my own land."

"Well then, you must do what you feel is right. Follow your conscience. I'm so proud - Ow!"

"Father, what is it?" cried Pia, as Kit slumped over the table, grabbing his left arm. "Father, Father. You're white as a sheet."

Kit didn't answer. He just lay there, ashen, and moaned as he held on to his arm, occasionally running his hand up to his jaw. Finally he spoke, in almost a whisper. "Lily, call Lily. Get one of the men to help me to the drawing room so I can lie down."

Pia screamed for help. Lady Cynthia's butler hurried into the room, and immediately saw what was happening. "Help him to the drawing room. Lay him on the sofa. I'm ringing my mother immediately." Pia ran to the telephone in the hallway and gave the operator Lily's number. In just a moment her calm voice was on the line, and Pia began to weep hysterically. "Lily, Lily, come at once. Kit has collapsed. He's holding his left arm and rubbing his jaw. I'm no doctor, but I would bet he's having a heart seizure. He was complaining of indigestion only a few minutes ago."

Lily didn't wait to hear any more. She just said "I'm on my way," and hung up immediately. Turning to John, who was standing in the hallway, she said, "John, I need you. I think Kit's had a heart seizure. That was Pia. You must run me to the house in your auto."

Together they ran from the surgery, both carrying their black medical bags. John drove like a bat out of Hell, and they were at Claybourne Court in less than five minutes. He screeched to a halt in front of the Dower House, and the two of them ran to the door. They didn't stop to knock, but ran inside and straight to the drawing room, since Pia had indicated that's where he would be. As they entered the room, they saw Kit lying on the sofa, terribly pale, with a hand knitted blanket covering him and Pia sitting on the floor, smoothing back his hair. She was weeping.

"Here darling, you must move, so that John and I can get to him. I need to check his blood pressure and his pulse rate. Oh good, you've loosened his collar," Lily said, as she wrapped the cuff of the pressure monitor around his arm. His eyes were closed, and he was shaking. John produced a small vial of nitroglycerin tablets and placed one under Kit's tongue. Lily's eyes looked extremely alarmed as she read the pressure. His pulse rate was equally worrisome. Lily tried to speak to him, and finally he opened his eyes.

"Lily, is that you? I can hear you, but my vision is very blurred. I feel like you're far away."

"Hang on, Kit. We need to get you to hospital. You need oxygen and more care then we can provide here. Please try to hang on, darling. John is calling for the ambulance lads. It will only be a tick. I love you, Kit. I need you. Please don't leave me. You're my life."

"Yes... my life, too. Always... my life... Lily? Lily?"

"Oh God, Kit. Please don't leave me. Please. Stay with me. We need each other."

"Lily... a light.... Have to go... not afraid.... love you..."

Kit's head fell to the side, and he closed his eyes for the last time. Lily leaned forward and put her head on his heart. She could hear no pulse. She placed her fingers on the sides of his neck. Again, there was no pulse. He was gone. Kit was gone. She put her head on his chest again and began to sob. Grasping his shirt, she balled up some fabric in her hand and cried until it was soaked through. She could hear the sirens from the ambulance pulling into the drive. John came back into the room, and she raised her head. "Tell them they can turn the sirens off, John. It's too late. We've lost him," she said, as she looked at her husband's still body, tears streaming down her face.

John, who had never let his emotions get the best of him in any situation, whether it was during the war or in the many years that he'd practiced medicine, broke down as well. "Oh God, Lily. Oh my God. I loved him like a brother. How can this have happened? Why didn't I see it coming? He's been under so much stress."

Lily never dreamed she would be in the position of having to alleviate the pain of her medical partner and dear friend because of the sudden death of her beloved husband. Finally they ended up trying to comfort one another. Pia ran to the telephone and rang Gena. Wearily John got up and took the telephone. He explained what had happened, and she asked what she could do to help. John told her to meet them at the hospital, where Kit would be taken by ambulance. Then Lily would have to make the hard decisions regarding the myriad of details that would follow. First, Lady Cynthia had to be notified. So did Win, Jordan, the staff, Lily's own mother and the newspapers. Lily knew she had to be strong, and those natural instincts kicked into gear. She stood on shaky legs, wiped her eyes and asked Mrs. Briggs to find Win and Jordan, and bring them to her.

7

T he light went out of Lily's life. She would have liked to curl up into a ball and pull the covers over her head, shutting out what was left of her world. But that wasn't even a remote possibility. She had children and needed to set an example for them. She had a medical surgery, and her income was a vital part of what was needed to keep the family solvent. So she carried on, although there were days and even weeks that were a blur in her mind.

Following the funeral in the Claybourne Chapel, Kit was laid to rest in the burying ground on the property. Lily visited his grave daily, and it was never without flowers. It seemed so unfair that he had died so young. She recalled that his father had also passed before his time. Now Win was suddenly the new earl, having not even reached his majority. He wouldn't be twenty-one until 1936, which left Lily in the position of overseeing the estate as his guardian. She relied heavily upon Henson, who was like a savior. She made frequent trips to London to meet with financial advisors and was glad to learn that because of the many safeguards that had been implemented at the beginning of the Great Slump, Claybourne Court was free of any encumbrance. She was advised to continue with the mill's operation, which it turned out later was the best decision she might have made.

Once again the family came to her aid, just as they had in 1929. Win, of course, was devastated. At first he didn't want to return to Oxford, but Lily insisted. She knew Kit would have been adamant that his son finish his education. Pia said that she, too, would return to Claybourne Court and lend assistance to Lily, but that was immediately ruled as unacceptable. Lady Cynthia was a brick, and any residue of bad feeling between them was completely laid to rest. Kit's mother had been amazed at Lily's strength when Kit had faltered in 1929, and she had grown steadily more admiring of her daughter-in-law's courage and fortitude during the ensuing years.

Although she wasn't without the support of those who loved her, Lily felt as though something had died within her. She carried on and did what was necessary, even smiled and laughed when it was appropriate, but her heart was shattered. At the end of each day she retreated to her room and shut out the world. The grief was overwhelming. She couldn't imagine ever truly being happy again. She had terrible guilt feelings about the time she and Kit had been separated, and even questioned whether she had done the correct thing when she left and went to medical school. Although her success and skill had carried them though an awful patch, she wished she could go back to that time and recapture the years that were lost, time she might have spent with Kit.

Finally she did what she had done so often in the past. She took her troubles to her friend and business partner, John Garrett, and to Gena, John's wife and Lily's closest friend. One morning before patients began to arrive, she asked if Gena and John could spare a moment. They immediately sat down in her office.

"The two of you have been my bricks so many times in my life. I know that I appear to be all right on the outside, but I feel dead inside. I need help, but I can't imagine anything that would make me feel like life is worth living," Lily began.

"Lily, you've been though one of the most horrible ordeals life can throw at a person," answered Gena. "What you're feeling is normal. I know, as a physician, many times you've had to explain the grieving process to patients, but when the topic pertains to you it's an entirely different thing to sort out."

"It's only been a little over a year, Lily. Part of you is still in shock. It was a dreadful, unexpected loss. Kit seemed so vital. You're going through the worst phase of grief, depression and loss of ability to see anything ahead but purposeless days of sorrow. It's normal, Lily. No one can speed up the process, and there is no way to avoid it. You can't go over it, under it, or around it. You have to experience this, and believe me, you will eventually come out the other side all the stronger for it. Focus on your children. They have always been the light of your life, and of Kit's." John always had a calming, reassuring manner. His advice had helped her many times, from the trauma of the battlefields in France, to the rocky path her marriage had taken when she left and went to medical school.

"John, I know what you're saying is right. I know it intellectually, but I can't find my emotional bearings. I'm feeling terribly guilty. I feel that I never should have left Kit. We lost so many years together. Now I believe we could have worked things out, without such a long time apart. I wonder if I didn't manufacture a reason to leave, because I wanted so much to be a doctor."

John surprised her with his answer. "I've thought for a long time that's exactly what you did. Now, don't misunderstand me. I don't for a moment think that you fabricated things that happened, that forced you to feel you could no longer live with Kit. But yes, there was always your great desire to become a doctor. When the path got rocky, there was the enticement of another avenue. I have to say that I think it's very fortunate that there was. If you had stayed with Kit, I don't believe things would have righted themselves. A break was needed. Kit needed to see things and to sort through what his true beliefs were, what sort of man he wanted to be. I rather doubt he would have done that unless there had been a period of separation. I also rather doubt that you would ever have been happy living an unfulfilled life, even if Kit had been the absolute paragon that you had him made out to be in the beginning. In the end, when you came back together, you were both certain of who you were as individuals, and of what you needed in a marriage. You might have had those years together, but I don't believe they would have been happy. Now you would be left bereft with absolutely nothing in your life. You have the thing you have always loved better than anything, Lily. You have medicine. It's been the center of your being since you were a small girl. Use it now. You have always believed that God has strange ways of leading us where we need to go. Perhaps there's a hidden plan that none of us can understand in what seems to be such a cruel blow. Think about that, Lily."

Lily was silent for a long while. She sat looking at the floor, tracing the pattern of the carpeting in her office. Finally she spoke. "You know, John. You may be right. I hadn't thought of Kit's death that way. But yes, I have always believed that things happen for a reason. It's awfully hard to fathom what reason there could be, but perhaps if I wait and have patience, time will show that this was God's plan for me. I remember when I joined the Voluntary Aid Detachment back in 1916. If I hadn't erroneously believed that Kit wanted to reconcile with Eleanor, I never would have made such a decision. But as it turned out, it was one of the most beneficial experiences in my life. I came away from there having met you and Gena, and with much, much greater maturity. That's true of so much of my life, when I think carefully. Even my father's death, which signaled the end of my educational dreams and having to go out to work, led me to Claybourne Court, Kit, Win, Pia, Jordan and all of the things that mean the most to me now."

"Do you see how the pathway winds, Lily? Sometimes we're wounded to the core by life's events, but if we wait, and have faith, new pathways emerge. Look at Gena and me. When I met her, I had lost the girl I thought was the love of my life. When she was killed, I vowed that I would never feel love again. I didn't believe it was remotely possible. While Anna, my deceased fiancé was a wonderful human being, Gena filled the hole in my heart and I can't imagine that I might have been as happy with anyone else."

Gena smiled at John. "Lily, John's right. The most important thing you need to have now is hope. Just a small glimmer of hope. It's much too soon to expect that you'll recover from this horrible tragedy, but if you'll concentrate on the things you still have, your medical practice, your children, and your lovely home that Kit so dearly loved, I believe in time you'll learn how to be happy again. Lily, life is really a series of deaths. As we grow, we move from one stage to another. Life is about growth."

"I know you're right. I need to readjust my thinking. I'm aware that it's going to be a long, slow, painful process, but I have so much help. I'm so much more fortunate than many, and I need to keep that uppermost in my mind. I loved Kit with all of my heart, but I need to be grateful for the time we did share together instead of being angry that I didn't have more." Again, there was silence. "Thank you so much. Thank you for listening, and thank you for always being here for me, through good and bad times. Just talking to you both has helped me to see things in a clearer light and from a different perspective. I'll muddle through until God decides to present me with more paths and more growth." Tears welled in Lily's eyes, and one slipped down her cheek. "I love you both so much," she murmured.

"We're here for you, Lily, whenever you need to talk. Life is a strange series of twists and turns, but it's those same bends and curves that make it interesting. None of us would like to live a straight line. It would be pretty boring, wouldn't it? How could there ever be happiness, if we didn't know what sadness was?" John pondered.

❦

Lily took their advice to heart. Her pain didn't ease, and the loneliness was sometimes unbearable. But a bit of hope *did* emerge, and she learned new patience, believing that life would eventually get better. The economy didn't improve much, but at least in their part of England it didn't worsen either. The medical surgery continued to thrive, and Lily was thankful for the fact that she was incredibly busy. All of her children were home for every holiday, but they weren't terribly merry times. There were no Christmas galas, which stopped at the beginning of the slump. Still it was nice to have Win and Pia join her and Jordan.

In 1936 their new King, Edward VIII, abdicated the throne on December 6 to marry his American paramour. It had been a monumental happening, and England was now starting to pick up the pieces with a new king, Edward's brother, George, and his lovely wife Elizabeth. With their two little girls, Lilibet and Margaret Rose, they made a very nice family and presented a fine image for the country. The abdication had been the topic of the moment in the country, and Claybourne Court was no different than any other in that regard. It was the conversation that dominated Christmas dinner. Pia had met the infamous Mrs. Simpson and had kinder feelings for her than most people, but Win was disgusted with the former king and was glad that the crisis had reached an end. Jordan, at eleven years, thought it was quite a romantic scandal. The year was also significant because Win turned twenty-one in April. It had been over two years since Kit's death, and Lily was coming to terms with her new position in life. She still dressed in black, although it wasn't expected of her, but she also showed a brighter attitude. Her patients could see it in her manner. Win would complete his years at Oxford in June of 1937. Lily knew how proud his father would have been to see his son become a man and taking his place in the long line of gentry who'd kept Claybourne Court enduring and progressing through the ages. Lily had been a splendid steward of his inheritance, and as soon as he finished his studies, he planned on taking the helm at Claybourne Court. Lily and the entire family attended his graduation exercises at Oxford, and they all returned immediately to Claybourne-on-Colne. Susie Gatewood was among those who watched the tall, handsome young man, who so resembled his father, walk across the stage to collect his diploma. He had been an outstanding student, graduating with a first-class honors degree. Lily was so proud. Lady Cynthia cried for one of the few times that Lily could remember, and Lily did something equally rare, placing her arms about her mother-in-law. Lady Cynthia completely broke down, putting her head on Lily's shoulder.

"Lily, I'm so proud of Win and can't help but think about when I sat here so many years ago watching his father complete this chapter of his life. Don't let Win see me weep. I don't want anything to spoil his perfect day."

"It's all right, Mother Claybourne. Everyone cries at graduations," Lily smiled. "Just remember that Win has accomplished what Kit wanted for him, so feel happy, not sad. Kit wouldn't want that."

"Lily, I'm so sorry I misjudged you years back. I marvel at your strength. You've been an inspiration to all of us, and if it hadn't been for you we might have lost Claybourne Court. Please forgive me for my foolishness. It takes longer for some of us to wake up and admit mistakes. I'm proud of you too, Lily."

Lily was stunned. She never thought she'd hear those words from Lady Cynthia's mouth. "I've only done what anybody would do under the circumstances we were faced with," she answered. "I learned about strength from you, Mother Claybourne. It was you who taught me how to be a countess. Don't ever forget that. I know we've had our differences, but that was long ago, and I was also to blame."

Lady Cynthia hugged Lily back. "God Bless you, Lily. I pray that you'll find happiness again in your life."

When everyone returned to Claybourne Court, Mary had arranged a lovely party for Win. John, Gena, Will, Elisabeth, David and Jane Morris, as well as the Claybourne family gathered to celebrate Win's achievements. Henson was present, and Win told him that he intended to begin accompanying him on daily rounds of the estate, learning all he needed in order to eventually manage his inheritance. Win also intended to work for several weeks in the Claybourne Mill, acquiring hands-on experience, so that he could be in a position to make intelligent decisions in the future. Susie stood at his side gazing at him with pride and love, and Lily wondered if they would be announcing their marriage shortly. Susie had finished her nurse's training and was working at the hospital in Claybourne-on-Colne. When they were married, there would have to be a discussion about reopening Claybourne Court. Whether Lily would live there too was up in the air. Normally she would have moved into the Dower House when her son took the reins as the Earl of Gloucester, along with Susie becoming his countess, but Lady Cynthia was still living. If Claybourne Court were reopened, Lily felt quite strongly that Lady Cynthia deserved to spend time to herself, since all through the slump years she had been so good about opening her doors to Lily and Jordan, not to mention Win and Pia when they were home.

Lady Cynthia was in her mid-seventies, but still a handsome lady. She didn't show her years. She had slowed down a bit, but Lily often wondered if that was due more to the financial conditions that prevailed in the Claybourne household, than to a loss of energy on her part. In fact, Lily had been somewhat surprised when Lady Cynthia ran into an old friend at Oxford, the Duke of Wexford, Aubrey Belmont. He was a widower who had once been close friends with Kit's father. When he saw Lady Cynthia, he seemed delighted, as did she. He invited her to a weekend house party in the summer months, and she had readily accepted.

So the summer progressed. Win was exceedingly busy with his plans to learn everything* he needed to become an exemplary steward of Claybourne Court. Lily worked long hours at the surgery, and Pia starred in two blockbuster movies in England, after signing a new contract with a British studio. *Flames over England* became one of the most successful pictures of its time. She continued to work hard and made back-to-back films. Lily was terribly proud of her, but wondered if she would ever marry. She was thirty-four years old, long past the age that most women did marry and have children. Her single state had nothing to do with a lack of attention from gentlemen, as she was always seen on the arm of one or another. The only answer she gave when asked if she would someday want to marry was that she had never met anyone who interested her enough. Lily sighed, but she knew that Pia had always marched to the beat of a different drummer.

In November of 1937, an incident occurred which very few people had any knowledge about. Many years later it would become a well-known fact. On November 5, what later became known as the Hossbach Conference, was held by Adolph Hitler. It was a secret meeting held at the Reich Chancellery. The people attending this conference, besides Adolph Hitler, were his foreign minister, the commanders in chief of the army, navy and Luftwaffe, and the minister of war. During this meeting Hitler laid out his plans for what eventually became World War II.

When 1938 arrived, echoes of that secret meeting began to reverberate. On March 12, Germany announced Anschluss, or Union, with Austria. Very quickly thereafter a brutal crackdown on Jewish people began. It became apparent that England needed to be gravely concerned that another war could be on the horizon. Win thought long and hard and spoke to anyone he felt could give him proper advice about how to proceed. When the German military mobilized on August 12, 1938, his decision was made.

Win volunteered and joined the army. He was first sent to the Royal Military Academy at Woolwich. He chose to be a Royal Engineer, and in order to do so, he would need to graduate in the top eighteen of cadets. Win had no difficulty reaching that goal, and as he left to actually take command of a section of soldiers, he was designated a second lieutenant. Lily hated to see him go. It reminded her vividly of his father leaving to join the Royal Scots Greys in 1914. There was no active war at the time, but rumors abounded.

Prime Minister Chamberlain traveled to Munich and returned on September 30, saying that he had accomplished "Peace in our time". But it was not to be. Almost a year to the date later, Britain, France, Australia, and New Zealand declared war on Germany. The lead up was slow, but steady.

First, on October 15, 1938, Hitler's army occupied Sudeten, the portion of Czechoslovakia inhabited by some three million Germans. Next a terrible event took place in Germany, which became known as *Kristallnacht*, one of the first blatant actions of the Nazis against the Jews. On November 9, 1938, a well-coordinated, gigantic attack against Jewish shops, department stores and synagogues took place. The "night of the broken glass" referred to the smashing of glass windows in Jewish owned businesses and homes. Some twenty-five thousand Jews were deported and many were sent on to concentration camps. There was shock and outrage throughout the world, and the United States recalled its ambassador permanently. On March 15 the Nazis took Czechoslovakia, and it became clear that war was inevitable. In August the British fleet mobilized and evacuations began in London. Lily straightened her back, took a deep breath and began to pray fervently for the safety of the young man she had held in her arms when he took his first lungful of air.

8

In fear of German bombs, children were queued up to be evacuated from London in a government program known as "Operation Pied Piper". Almost two million children were involved. Those sad little souls had no idea where they were going, nor who would care for them. They were given a postcard addressed to their London home and told to post it when they reached their destination.

In the midst of all the chaos, war was declared on September 3. Win continued to change locales as he traveled with the army along the coastal regions, working to shore up defenses in preparation for the real possibility that Germans would make an attempt to invade their isolated island. Before the end of October, Canada had joined the fight. Poland was defeated when Warsaw surrendered to the Nazis, and the Germans began to practice euthanasia on the sick and disabled. There was much worse to come.

However, more and more citizens began to call it the "Phony War". They were issued gas masks, bomb shelters were constructed and a Home Guard was activated. Although there was sea action involving the Royal Navy, nothing of much import happened in England. People began to get restless and wondered if the whole thing was false, that there wouldn't really be a war. A large number of parents brought their children back to London.

In the meantime, as spring approached, the tide turned. On April 9, 1940, the Germans attacked Norway and Denmark. After months of training in the homeland, Win was shipped to France with his unit. They crossed the English Channel and landed at Calais, where they were then transported by train to the city of Arras, north of Paris. Further down, in a village called St. Quentin, Win commanded his men to begin digging trenches on either side of the road which led to Arras. Arras was the French headquarters of the British Army.

On May 10, 1940, the same day that the Nazis broke through the lines of defense at Sedan, France, Winston Churchill became Prime Minister. Win received orders to begin a retreat forty miles back to the coastline, for a return to England. Thus, he and his troops began a long trek with German Luftwaffe airplanes flying overhead, with frequent interruptions to camouflage themselves behind hedgerows and trees to escape strafing. When they finally returned to the beaches at Dunkirk, they were unprepared for the gruesome sight awaiting them. Thousands of soldiers were standing, lying, and floating in the water which had turned red from their bloodshed. All were waiting for the chance to board a ship that would take them home to England. Not only were there men from their own army, but there were French soldiers, too. In addition, there were many refugees who had left their homes in small French villages, hoping to escape the onslaught of the Nazi army. As Win stood on the shore at Dunkirk, he scanned the horizon and saw Royal Air Force planes flying up and down the coastline, trying to give cover to the men who awaited transportation. German planes dive bombed over the beach area, cutting down soldiers with every pass. The Luftwaffe and the Royal Air Force engaged in countless dogfights in the skies above the English Channel. When night fell, hundreds of smaller boats joined the larger battleships in the attempt to rescue soldiers. It was an amazing sight. From poor fishermen in small dinghies to wealthy aristocrats in fancy yachts, they lined up to take their boys home. While Win awaited rescue, a low flying Luftwaffe plane caught him in the left shoulder with a direct hit. Blood began to pour from the wound, and Win hoped it hadn't hit an artery. He immediately shed his tunic and tore his shirt. Taking the strip of cloth, he wrapped it above the wound, effectively designing a makeshift tourniquet which staunched the bleeding as he stood in the cold night air, up to his knees in water, feeling disoriented. One of his mates saw the incident and came to his aid. Grabbing his canteen from the inside of his uniform, he gave Win water. He put his arm about Win's waist and tried to steady him. It was no place to pass out, nor to die. There was no system organized for soldiers to board the various rescue crafts, and it seemed to be haphazard. On some portions of the beach, numbers were being given out and the operation was a bit more orderly, but where Win was located, there was no such scheme and he was too weak to cover the distance to where things were running more smoothly. John Bannister, his fellow section mate, stayed by him and promised not to leave him until he was safely aboard a rescue craft. At long last a rather nice sized pleasure boat came near their spot. They gratefully accepted the help from the pilot of the yacht and were pulled abroad. Win lay down below deck and closed his eyes. There was a first aid kit on board, and other soldiers attended to his wound as best they could. He slept until the craft reached land at Dover. When he raised his head and looked out of the window, he was able to see the iconic white cliffs of which his father had spoken so long ago. Now he knew from personal experience what it felt like to see them and to know that he had returned to English soil. The craft was shelled as they left Dunkirk, and bombs were dropped near them on the way back to Dover. When they disembarked at Dover, they were crammed into trains. Win had no idea where he was going, and he didn't care very much. He was just grateful to be back on English soil. Occasionally the train stopped at wayside stations and kind, compassionate ladies offered sandwiches and tea. They were also given a postcard to address to their next of kin. Later he learned that his postcard was mailed to Lily, telling her that he had survived the ghastly ordeal at Dunkirk. He finally ended up at a camp in Hampshire where his shoulder was tended to properly. After that, all of the men were given a week's leave.

Word quickly spread throughout England about the incredible feat. The homeland speedily mobilized to support those who were rescued. Claybourne Court stood to be counted as a hospital for wounded and exhausted men. There were several landed estates in the country that were doing the same thing. Harewood House, in West Yorkshire, was another magnificent country house that volunteered to be utilized as a recuperation facility. The Lascelle family, who lived at Harewood, had volunteered their home in World War I as well. The government supplied military personnel to perform the necessary medical tasks, and Lily set about moving the family living quarters to one wing of the estate. All of Claybourne Court's other rooms were given over to the military for use in the recuperation of soldiers. The drawing room became a canteen where meals could be served to the ambulatory, and other large rooms became wards. The day before patients began to arrive, a convoy of nurses, doctors, and other medical personnel appeared. Lily graciously showed them their accommodations. The officer in charge of the operation was Colonel Bradley Barton, a staunchly professional gentleman with greying temples and a warm smile. He shook Lily's hand firmly, and thanked her profusely for allowing the military to make use of her home. He gave his word that it would be left in the condition in which it was found.

Lily laughed when she heard his name. "How ironic," she exclaimed. "My maiden name was Barton. Of course, it's a terribly common name, so I don't suppose there is a chance that we're related."

"How interesting," he replied. "No, I rather think not. Unless you have kin on the Channel Islands. That's where my ancestry originates."

"Truthfully, I've no idea," smiled Lily. "I suspect not, however. I grew up here, in Claybourne-on-Colne, and my father was from London originally. I believe my grandfather was from the Kent region. Still, it's interesting, isn't it?"

"Quite," he answered. "We'll have to take time for tea someday, and look at our ancestry more closely."

Lily agreed, and then offered to do whatever she could to make the transition easier for the staff of what would become a new convalescent hospital. Colonel Barton was pleased to learn that Lily herself was a physician, which he felt helped her to understand the needs of such a facility. Lily said she was pleased to be able to lend support to her country and that she would do all she could to help. She explained that her own medical practice kept her away from the estate during the daytime hours. Lily introduced him to Susie, the other staff and Jordan, when he returned from school at the end of the day.

In the midst of the chaos, Win arrived home for his furlough. Lily was stunned and delighted when she saw him walk through the doors. But when she saw his arm in a sling and a bandage on his shoulder, like any mother, she grew distressed. After being careful not to squeeze his shoulder when she embraced him, she stood back and fearfully asked him what had happened. Win explained the horror of the Dunkirk evacuation, which of course Lily knew about. In all, over three hundred and thirty-eight thousand soldiers from both the British Expeditionary Forces as well as the French military were brought back to England. However, while it was hailed as a miracle in terms of the rescue, it was still a horrible loss and Churchill said that "Wars are not won by evacuations".

Win was surprised to see all of the activity taking place at his ancestral home, but heartily agreed with Lily when given the details of the plan for Claybourne Court. They walked to the library and settled themselves comfortably. It was one of the few rooms left for the family's leisure. Before Win escaped to spend time with Susie, Lily wanted to take advantage of his unexpected visit to discuss an idea that had come to her just after war had been declared.

"Win, I've had an idea. I need to hear what your thoughts are. I may be totally off the rails in my thinking, but then again, it would be a tremendous windfall for Claybourne Court."

"What in blazes are you talking about?" Win smiled.

"I'm referring to the possibility of the Claybourne Mill procuring a contract with the Armed Forces to provide woolen fabric for uniforms. Does that even seem feasible? I know that some are constructed of wool."

"Absolutely, Mum. What a brilliant idea. They may have already awarded contracts, but there are going to be thousands of uniforms needed, so it would certainly be worth looking into."

"Who would I have to speak with about that sort of request?"

"I'm not certain. Why don't you talk to the colonel in charge here, this Barton fellow? As a colonel, I'd think he would at least know the procedure you'd need to follow. I think it's a smashing idea and could be extremely lucrative for Claybourne Mill."

"I think so, too, Win. I'll try to get some information from Colonel Barton. Now, I know you're chomping at the bit to see Susie. I believe she's on the second level, helping to prepare private rooms for more seriously wounded chaps."

"You're a pip, Mum, Win smiled, as he got up and kissed her on the cheek. "If you don't know it, I hope you realize how proud Dad would be of you," he added.

"Thank you, Win. I think he would be, too. Now run off to Susie."

After Win left, Lily searched the house until she came upon Colonel Barton. "Sir, may I have a moment of your time?" she asked.

"Of course, Lady Claybourne. How can I be of help?" he asked.

Lily explained her idea to him, and he told her that he thought it was a very intelligent goal. He suggested that Lily contact an officer who was the head of Supply Requisition based at the War Offices. Lily thanked him profusely and immediately went to the telephone to ring the correct department and make an appointment to speak with the recommended officer.

When Lily returned to Claybourne Court, after her visit to the War Department, she carried with her a copy of the contract she'd signed to produce an enormous amount of woolen fabric for the production of uniforms for all three branches of the military. It meant the end to belt-tightening at Claybourne Court. Her parents could stop paying for Jordan's schooling, and Pia could stop sending half of her pay to the family. It was a huge windfall. Win was delighted at her news. She called together everyone else, including the servants and farmers, to announce the end of financial difficulties at Claybourne Court. Of course at the same time, rationing went into effect, so while money wasn't as scarce as it had been, there were either no goods to purchase, or one needed rationing coupons to do so. Still, to be free of worry about such things as taxes, and even whether or not the mill could be kept operating, was a tremendous weight off Lily's shoulders.

A letter was waiting for Lily when she returned home. It was from Pia. She wanted news of Win, and she also mentioned that she would have time to come to Claybourne-on-Colne in the next week. All cinemas were being closed, and her studio had cancelled any films that were scheduled for production. She wrote that she was going to be traveling to several Royal Air Force stations in the next week. She would be visiting RAF Churchstanton in Somerset, and RAF Filton in Gloucestershire, among others. These last two camps were not a long distance from Claybourne-on-Colne, so she thought she would end her day with a stopover at home for several days, if not longer. These visits to military stations had begun when war was declared and were designed to keep morale high among soldiers and airmen. Many of Pia's co-stars made such outings, too.

Lily folded the letter and placed it back in its envelope. She hoped that Win's visit would overlap by at least a day.

As it turned out, Pia's letter had been delayed by the larger volume of mail due to the war footing. Later, on the same day the letter had arrived, so did Pia. She was glowing and seemed filled with happiness, which Lily hadn't expected. There was little to be happy about when the country was fearful that there would be Germans parachuting into their high streets at any moment. But after sitting down and having a chat with Pia, it became abundantly clear why her demeanor was one of elation.

When Pia had arrived at RAF Filton, a very impressive group captain met her and welcomed her to the camp. He seemed to be around Pia's age and was extraordinarily good-looking, in a rugged but refined manner. Pia said he wasn't at all "full of himself", was obviously competent and carried himself with esteem. The moment she'd set eyes upon him, she was smitten. His name was Group Captain Clayton Marshall. After she shook the hands of virtually every airman stationed at RAF Filton, Pia and Clay, as he was known, had gone to the Officers' Mess for a cup of tea. They ended up chatting for nearly three hours, and she felt as though she'd learned everything about him. According to her, he had joined the Royal Air Force in 1933, and trained at RAF Cranwell. He served in Training Command and as a flying instructor at RAF Montrose. He was stationed at RAF Tangmere in 1937 and was a member of Number 43 Squadron RAF. The first enemy aircraft to crash on English soil during World War II, fell victim to fighters from RAF Acklington on February 3, 1940, when the Hurricanes of 'B' flight, Number 43 Squadron shot down a Heinkel 111 near Whitby. Clay Marshall was one of the pilots. He had earned the Victoria Cross for this action. Pia described him as witty, kind, and obviously intelligent. In short, she was one step away from being head-over-heels for him.

This was completely unlike anything Lily had ever encountered with Pia. There was never a love interest. She'd had countless admirers and might have had anyone she'd set her cap at, but she had only concentrated upon her career. Now, all of that seemed to have changed.

"Pia, surely you can't be telling me that you've fallen in love with this RAF pilot, whom you scarcely know!" Lily exclaimed.

"Y-e-e-e-s Lily, I believe I have."

"But, darling girl, you don't really know him. What you've given me is a recitation of his attributes and accomplishments, which I agree are quite impressive. But you don't know him. Oh Pia, I fear you're doing something similar to what I did. You have to spend time knowing someone. You can't just race off head over tail. Look at the problems Kit and I ran into as a result of not having known each other properly."

"Lily, it all turned out in the end. The world has changed. There is a war. We don't have time to think about what could happen in ten years. I'm much older than you were. I'm not an innocent young girl. I've had my career. I've done it backward from you. Clay isn't a child either. We know what we feel. We believe we're soulmates."

"Oh my God, Pia. Do you mean to say that he feels this way about you, too?"

"Yes, he does. And, before you say it's only because I'm the great film star, Pia Claybourne, don't bother. If anything, he wishes that weren't the case. He was worried about that aspect, but I told him that I was willing to give up my career. I'm tired of acting other people's lives. I want to live my own."

"Pia, you're an adult. You've always been quite stubborn about doing what you want to do. I'm not going to interfere now. I remember what it's like to be in love. If this is what you want, then of course I'll support you in your decision. I just hope you'll wait a short while."

"Lily, I can't promise how long we'll wait. I haven't even kissed him yet, which I know sounds very strange. But I know, I just know, that he's the man I've been waiting for. I'll be here at Claybourne for two weeks, and I intend to drive over to RAF Filton as often as possible. If I can, I want to bring him here to meet you. But prepare yourself, Lily. I promise you.

Sooner or later I'm going to marry Group Captain Clayton Marshall." With that last statement, Pia scampered off to see her brother, Win.

9

Lily put her head in her hands. There was just so much happening, and her head was spinning. What would Kit say about Pia's escapade? She rubbed her temples. Tears filled her eyes as she thought about how much easier life would be if she still had her husband with whom to discuss problems. As she sat there, feeling alone, Colonel Barton rapped on the woodwork at the entrance to the library. The door was open, so he could clearly see that she was troubled. She raised her head and a tear escaped, falling down her cheek. She brushed it away with the back of her hand.

"Lady Claybourne, I'm sorry if I'm interrupting you. I can come back another time if you wish," he murmured, somewhat embarrassed.

"No, no. That's fine, sir. I've just been speaking with my eldest child, my step-daughter. It was a rather curious conversation." She gave him a watery smile.

"Would it help if you spoke with someone?" he asked.

"You know, it just might. I'm so tired of dealing with everything by myself. There really is nothing I can do in this instance. She's well past the age when I have any business giving her orders. It's just terribly hard to see them grow up and have to sit by and witness possible mistakes. Have you any children, Colonel Barton?"

"No, Lady Claybourne, I don't. I was married young, in 1914, just when the Great War began. We were together such a scant time. After the war, in 1918, she came down with that deadly flu, and I lost her. I've never re-married. I should have liked to, but I've never been in one place long enough, or so it seems. I was in India and then Burma and now we're up against the Germans again." He laughed, ruefully. "Perhaps someday, I'll find myself without a war and in England long enough to meet someone. I'm not certain what help I can be with advice on child-rearing, but I've been told I have a good listening ear."

"Oh, Pia, that's my step-daughter's name, is well past anything dealing with child-rearing. She's in her thirties."

Colonel Barton had seated himself across from Lily. "Pia? An unusual name. Italian, is it? It seems I've heard it somewhere before."

"Yes. Pia Claybourne. She's quite a well-known cinema actress. Perhaps that's where you know of her."

"Ah, yes. I've even seen several of her films. So, she's your daughter? How amazing. She's certainly a beautiful creature."

"Yes, she is that. And a wonderful lady, too. She was born in Italy. My deceased husband was quite young when she was born." Lily saw no reason to add all of the details surrounding Pia's birth. "In any event, Pia has been with me since she was sixteen. I love her dearly, but, it seems she's gone over-the-moon about some RAF group captain whom she only met today! Can you imagine? As I said, she's not a child. But this isn't ordinary behavior from her. In fact, while she's had a never-ending amount of interest from men, given her beauty and fame, she's never shown more than simple friendship for any suitor. Now, after one meeting, she vows she's going to marry this chap."

"Well, that *is* something of a surprise. I'm not sure what I'd do or say. I suppose you have to let her live her life. As you say, she's not a child. Does she say whether this chap feels as she does?"

"Apparently he does. I'm trying to sort it all out. He's stationed at RAF Filton, not very far away. She says she's going to drive over there every day."

"I'd imagine that he's going to be a very busy chap quite soon. Now that the Nazis have taken Paris, I suspect their next move will be to aim their blasted Luftwaffe planes at London. Their goal will be to soften us up in preparation for an invasion. If that comes to pass, our fly boys will be the ones to handle the fight."

Lily's mind drifted to memories of Paris, when she'd been young, and unmarried. It was inconceivable that the German flag was flying in the Place de la Concorde. Nazis had entered Paris on June 10, 1940, and the world had been aghast to see that lovely city under German occupation. Colonel Barton was surely right. It was common knowledge that the Germans would turn their attention to creating as much havoc as possible in England. The long dreaded bombing of London was expected at any moment. Lily had heard from her friends Maddie and Poppy, whom she'd known since her days as a Voluntary Aid Detachment nurse in World War I, and who figured in her memories of Paris in 1917. Both friends were now married and living in London. They wrote of the constant air-raid sirens and worried about an attack. Lily had suggested that they evacuate to Claybourne-on-Colne, but it wasn't that simple. Their husbands both had employment concerns, and since nurses were in short supply they both felt needed in the capital. Lily quickly brought her thoughts back to the present as Colonel Barton continued.

"Do you have hopes of meeting this chap?" he asked.

"She said she'd like that," Lily replied. "I'm going to try to persuade her that she absolutely must bring him here before she makes any decision. Perhaps the war will slow their ardor."

"Or speed it up," he smiled. "Wars have a tendency to do that, you know. You didn't ask, but my advice would be not to argue against her feelings. If, as you say, this isn't common behavior for her, she surely believes she's in love with this chap. And perhaps she is. Stranger things have happened. Of course you know that to argue with someone whose gone over-the-moon like this would only serve to fan the flames. I imagine he's not a bad sort. The RAF is a splendid branch of the military, and as a group captain he certainly has to have shown his mettle."

"I'm actually not worried about that, Colonel. I just fear that because Pia is so well-known and really quite beloved by so many, it's possible that he's confusing his feelings. You know how people can become dewy-eyed, particularly over engaging film stars. In Pia's case, she's even more alluring in person. Not only is she just as exquisite looking as she is on film, but she has a sweet, demure way about her. I can understand why a man would find her hard to resist."

"Yes. There is that. I hope she brings him to meet you. I suspect she will, since it sounds as if you're very close. I rather think it's so much easier to gauge your feelings when you've actually met someone face-to-face. You seem to be a good judge of character," he smiled.

"I hope I am," Lily answered. "But actually, it doesn't much matter, does it Colonel? After all, regardless of what I think of him, it's Pia's life."

"Right you are, there. Life does have a way of sorting itself out though. I imagine that's what will happen in this case. I've often told myself to stop fretting, and give it to God. It's worked quite well, thus far." There was a short pause. "Well, I'd better get back to matters at hand, regarding the nursing facility. I expect we're going to start receiving patients very soon. That's what I came to tell you. I've had word that many of the London hospitals are discharging cases from the Dunkirk evacuation and sending them along for longer term recuperation. It's likely the London hospitals will be swamped with casualties from bombing raids soon."

"Is there anything I can do to help?" Lily asked. "Here I am worried about my own little troubles when England is facing such beastly and grave danger. There are my own patients to see. I have three expectant mothers who are due momentarily. What a nasty world to be bringing babies into," Lily murmured.

"Life continues, Lady Claybourne. I think there's something rather reassuring about that," he smiled.

"Yes. I agree," Lily replied. There was another moment of silence between them. "Colonel, since you're going to be here for a long spell, don't you think we should at least be on a first name basis?" she asked.

"Absolutely. Please, call me Bradley, or Brad"

"And I'm Lily. I expect we'll be having more conversations. Thank you for listening to my ramblings. I'm going to do as you said. I'm giving it to God. When I've done that in the past, it's never failed me."

Win left to report back to his station the following morning. He was quite secretive about where he would be, as well as the details about his mission. Lily understood his silence. Having lived through one war, she was familiar with military protocol. She held him tightly and wished him godspeed, then waved as Edward drove him to the station. He wouldn't allow her to accompany him, saying he always wanted to think of her at Claybourne Court and not a dreary rail depot. Susie was the only one allowed to be at his side until he boarded the train. They were totally committed to one another, and both had agreed that if the war continued and worsened, they would marry. Win had decided that if something should happen to him, he wanted Susie to receive the small pension to which he would be entitled. Susie only wanted to have the memory of having been his wife. For the time being they pledged to wait and see, but Susie kept an appropriate dress ready at all times in case the situation called for a sudden elopement.

After Win's departure Susie returned to Claybourne Court and dressed to report for her work as a nurse at the Claybourne Hospital. She ran into Pia in the hallway.

"You're up and dressed early, Pia. What are your plans for the day?" Susie asked.

"I'm driving over to RAF Filton. I want to see Clay before he's off on a sortie."

"Does he know to expect you?" asked Susie.

"Yes, we planned in advance. He'll be at the main gate of the airfield. I don't know how long I'll be able to stay, but anything is better than nothing. I'm going to speak to him about the possibility of his coming to Claybourne Court for a visit, to meet Lily and you."

"Oh, Pia! I would so love to meet him, and I know Lily would be thrilled. Do try to sort that out."

"I shall. But, I must be on my way now. Did Win get off all right? I know you're sad to see him go."

"Yes, I went to the station. I hate these goodbyes. I never know how long it will be before I see him again."

"I know. Thank God, so far there hasn't been as much ground war. But I'm sure his time will come. Enjoy what time you can with him."

"Oh, I do, Pia. We've decided that we'll probably marry before much longer, if this thing gets worse or just goes on and on. I don't want to wait any longer. I've loved him forever, and I want to be his wife."

"I understand that thinking perfectly. War isn't a time to sit around and dither about such things. There isn't time. You have to live for the moment and take your chance at happiness while you can."

"Oh, Pia, you sound as if you're thinking along the same lines. Are you?" Susie asked.

"Yes. I know it's sudden. Don't give me the 'Lily lecture'. But if we both love one another, and there's no impediment to marriage, which there isn't, why not cherish every moment we can have together?"

"Indeed," Susie responded. "Why not? I'll be saying a prayer for you, dear Pia. Do bring your group captain here to meet us."

"Perhaps today. We'll see," Pia replied.

They exchanged a hug, and the two young ladies went their separate ways.

Pia dressed conservatively, not wanting to look too glamorous and start tongues wagging upon her arrival at RAF Filton. She slipped on a pale yellow, cotton dress that came to just below her knees. Over that she wore a simple white cardigan. She tied her lovely hair back into a ponytail and wore very little makeup, some lip rouge and a little color on her cheekbones. Stepping back from the mirror she surveyed herself. She looked unworldly enough to be arriving at the RAF station like any other girlfriend or wife. How silly it all was. She was rather looking forward to saying goodbye to her film career and settling down as a normal English housewife. She was tired of having to look perfect every time she poked her head out of doors and of having the studio script her life. She'd enjoyed marvelous years, and had accomplished heights she'd never dreamed possible, but Pia wasn't the sort of girl who'd become wrapped up in all of the glitter and glamour of being a star. She was much too well-grounded for that. She'd always known she would someday leave her film career behind and return to the real world. The time appeared to be upon her.

When she arrived at RAF Filton, there was Group Captain Clay Marshall waiting at the entrance gate. He had taken care of the formalities involved with signing her in, and he slid into the seat beside her. Pia drove a 1940 black Aston Martin given to her by the studio. She loved her little car. It offered the freedom she longed for. She still had one year left on her cinema contract with a commitment to make two more films, but at the moment nothing was happening in the industry. All that was being asked was that she visit army, air, and naval stations throughout England to help with morale. *Well,* she thought to herself on that sunny summer morning, *I'm carrying out my duties by raising Clayton Marshall's morale.*

She looked over at him in his immaculate blue uniform with the wings on his jacket. Her heart did a somersault. Everything about him was so perfect. His brown hair had streaks of gold running through it, and there was even some grey at the temples, which only served to make him look more distinguished. Pia had always believed that eyes were the window to the soul, and she'd concentrated on his eyes when they'd first met. They were a very dark blue, with enormous intensity. Deep-set and penetrating, when he spoke, he never diverted from direct eye contact. Pia liked that trait. He had the skin tone that tanned easily in the summer months, unlike many of the British. Pia was a sun-lover, and with her Mediterranean skin she could afford to be. She had never burned in her life. She simply turned a lovely shade of deeper gold. It appeared that Clay was the same way. She envisioned afternoons pottering about a garden, both of them warmed by the sun, caring for the grounds of their own cottage someday. She already knew that they both loved the country and that neither wanted to live in a big city environment. She'd had her fill of that while based in both Los Angeles and London doing films. He, too, much preferred a country environment. They were both readers, and Pia already knew that they could spend hours keeping current with literature and discussing their thoughts.

Clay wanted children, but not too many. Pia agreed completely. Two, perhaps three at the most, they laughed. They were both Church of England Anglicans, so religion presented no issue. As a small girl in Italy, Pia had grown up as a Catholic, but when she'd come to Claybourne Court she had eventually converted to Anglicanism. There was scant difference in the service, yet she liked the easing of restrictions on some of the more worrisome beliefs of the Catholic Church, such a birth control. In short, at least on the surface, and also on a very preliminary basis, they seemed to be a match. However, Pia was intelligent enough to know that other more subtle differences could create havoc within what sometimes appeared to be a well-matched couple. She intended to sort everything out before any knots were tied, and since Clay was the sort who didn't generally act impulsively, he, too, was inclined to want to know every last thing about Pia before a final commitment was made. That meant spending as much time as possible together. They drove to the Officers' Club where Pia parked the auto. Then they went into the building, a temporary structure scarcely worthy of the name. However, they were able to get a good breakfast there. They drank tea and talked about plans for the day. Clay had put in for leave, and it had been granted. Things were expected to be rather slow for the next couple of weeks, and the RAF was going easy on its pilots in preparation for a monumental build-up when, and if, the Germans began their bombing campaign. When Pia heard that he'd been given so much free time, she immediately asked him if he would like to go to Claybourne Court to meet her family and to see where she'd grown up. He agreed at once.

By the end of the day they were in Claybourne-on-Colne, and Clay was raving about how quaint the village seemed, the England he had always dreamed about. He had been born in Burma when his father was serving there, having come from a military family. He'd spent all of his life on military stations, which didn't tend to be quaint, or charming. Pia's home was a bit daunting, and she could see from his face as she pulled up in front of its imposing edifice, that he felt a bit intimidated. She reached over and patted his hand. "My family are just people, Clay. Like any others. Don't worry. You'll love Lily, my stepmother. I did tell you she's a doctor didn't I? She's really a remarkable person. I've watched her grow from a pampered young countess into a very strong woman. She kept all of us afloat during the Great Slump. I admire her tremendously. I wish you could meet my father, but we lost him before the war. He was a dear man. I miss him every day, but if I'm perfectly honest, I think it's better that Lily was left behind, because she's so strong and determined. I'm not sure Father could have functioned as well as she has without her by his side. They were a good team, which is what I think marriage should be," Pia commented.

"I absolutely agree with you. I want a full partner. I can't imagine going through life making the terribly hard decisions without someone you love and trust being there beside you, making certain the correct conclusions are reached."

He just kept on saying the right things.

85

10

They found themselves in the massive great hall at Claybourne Court, with the second level balcony looking down upon them. Pia wished the drawing room had been in its usual condition, but it was war time and nothing could be done except ask Clay to envision what it looked like without long tables set up to serve staff and patients who were ambulatory. She showed him through the first level of the home, except for the rooms that had already been designated wards and had received recuperating patients. She found Lily in the library going over the accounts from her own business. She had been trying to spend a few more hours a day at the house while the transition was occurring, so she tried to make use of that time by concentrating on desk work she would normally have been doing at her surgery. She looked up, rather startled, when Pia and Clay entered the room. Lily was never a woman who had to worry about being caught off guard, with her hair undone, or dressed inappropriately. She began every day with the four inch bath that rationing allowed, and then dressed, usually in an attractive but simple twin set in the cooler months, or a conservative cotton or linen day dress in the summer. Her hair was always fashioned in an updo without a strand out of place. She'd never been given to the heavy use of color in cosmetics, but did use a pale pink lip rouge and the same shade on her cheek bones. Her brows were left natural, and the only other enhancement was a slight darkening on the tips of her naturally long lashes. She was still a beautiful woman at age forty-six. She did not come across as intimidating. There were shades of the old Lily, especially when she met someone who might be overawed by her title. She certainly knew that Group Captain Marshall would not be completely relaxed. If what Pia was telling her was correct, there was a lot riding on the impression he made.

He needn't have worried. Lily understood immediately why Pia was so smitten. They all sat down in the library, and Lily rang for a tea tray. In the meantime she opened the conversation by asking some general questions about Clay's background and experience. They weren't questions designed to make him feel as though he were undergoing an interrogation, but rather more designed to put him at ease.

"So, Captain Marshall, is that the correct way to address you? Pia tells me you're a group captain, but does one use the full title, or is captain alone sufficient?" she asked.

"Lady Claybourne, I'd be delighted if you'd address me as Clay or Clayton. Most everyone knows me as Clay."

"Then I shall do that, Clay. And of course, you must feel free to call me Lily."

"Oh, I don't think I'd feel comfortable with that so quickly," he replied. "Is there an in-between of sorts?" he smiled.

"Couldn't he call you 'Lady Lily', as some of the staff, like Mrs. Briggs do?" Pia broke in.

"That's fine with me, if he prefers it," answered Lily. "I'm just fine with Lily, but I agree it takes some getting used to, so if Lady Lily makes you feel better, let's proceed with that."

"Yes. I feel more comfortable with that," he responded.

"And you were born where, Clay? I don't remember if Pia told me. She rattled off a lot of details very quickly," Lily laughed.

"I was born on a military station in Burma. That's rather been the story of my life. I often tell people that I must have been born behind a moving lorry that was transporting our furnishings from one post to another. We never really had a true home until I was much older, and my Dad demobilized. Then we returned to England and lived in Wiltshire. That was my first taste of English life. I adore the country. Pia and I agree on that completely."

"The military life can be very difficult for children, can't it?" Lily replied.

"Yes, it can. I think there are pros and cons. I've seen a great deal of the world. My grades in geography were always well above average, for obvious reasons. But it's hard to be settled and then told it's time to move again. I think it probably contributes to a lack of security in children."

"Do you plan on following in your father's footsteps and making your career in the military?" Lily asked.

"No. I see unimaginable possibilities arising out of air travel. I believe those of us who get in on the ground floor, so to speak, will be in an excellent position to take advantage of those opportunities. I can see becoming a pilot for a commercial airline, or even holding an administrative position. There are already plans in the works for transatlantic passenger planes. I believe that someday an individual will be able to circle the globe by airplane. I want to be a part of that. I think with my success thus far, I'll have put myself in a good position to be considered for many different avenues in the aviation industry."

"How very exciting. I wish I were young again. There are going to be previously unknown fields opening up after this awful war."

"Yes, the war can't be negated. That's the first priority. Nothing can develop, and we can't move ahead until the enemy is defeated. But we're doing a bloody good job of holding our own. Excuse my language, Lady Lily, but I get somewhat passionate when I think of what the RAF has accomplished."

"As well you should," she smiled. "I know there are rumors of the bombing coming to England at long last. I imagine that means your branch of the service will be very heavily involved?"

"Yes, indeed. We've been practicing round the clock. Let them throw their best at us. I think they'll be surprised. We may be outnumbered, but we're superbly trained. In my opinion, there will never be a German invasion. They have us Brits all wrong. We'll fight as hard and as long as we have to. There won't be any capitulating, and no German flag will ever fly over the Houses of Parliament." His voice became very firm when he spoke those words.

"Well Clay, I must say I'm very impressed with you, and I can understand why our Pia seems to have gone a bit-over-the-moon. I don't think I'm telling any tales of out of school when I say that, am I?"

"No. No, Lily," answered Pia. "Clay and I are very open with each other about our feelings."

"Lady Lily, I think we need to get down to it. There is a thousand pound elephant in the room, and here we are, acting as though it doesn't exist. I know that you're concerned about the abruptness of our feelings for one another. I'm sure if I were a parent I would be, too. Perhaps I can ease your mind a bit. Pia isn't the only one over-the-moon. I'm not a child, Lady Lily. I'll be forty years old this autumn. I've known my share of women, but I've never remotely been in love the way I am with Pia. I know it's sudden. Everything today seems sudden. But Lady Lily, even if we had the luxury of a long courtship, followed by an equally long engagement, I don't expect for one moment that either Pia's or my feelings would change. We both sense that we've searched all of our lives for one another. I don't know if you believe in soulmates, Lady Lily, but both Pia and I do. There just doesn't seem to be any other explanation for the immediate attraction we felt. And before you even think that my feelings have anything to do with Pia's fame, please understand that I personally think that is rubbish. I'm not at all impressed with the fact that she is a film star. I've met film stars before. Most are vain, narcissistic creatures of whom I want no part. Pia is exactly what I knew the woman I'd fall in love with would be like. Her beauty is only one aspect of her being. There is a sweetness about her, consideration for the feelings of others and kindness. She has strong values and great faith. I believe we want the same things out of life. I think that each of us makes the other whole."

"It would be very difficult for me to find fault with anything you're saying," Lily replied. "The only thing I want is to see Pia happy. I've never believed she would stay in the film industry forever and have always thought that she would make a marvelous wife and mother. I warn you, though, she can be a stubborn little creature. If she gets something into her head, it's very difficult to stop her. Did she tell you about how she walked from Rome to England when she was sixteen years old?"

"We haven't got to all of my stories, Lily," Pia laughed. She turned to Clay. "I promise I'll tell you tonight. It all seems so long ago."

"It was long ago," said Lily. "But it's a perfect example of her determination. You'll need to keep that in mind."

"Are you giving us your blessing, Lady Lily?" Clay asked.

"I believe I am. What else am I to do? You're obviously in love, and neither one of you is a child. I have to trust that you know your own hearts. Of course I'll worry a bit, that's a mother's prerogative, and you must promise me that if the path gets rocky, you won't run away at the first sign of difficulty. I think you two just may have hit upon something here. You do seem inordinately well-suited to one another, and I've no doubt that the chemistry is right. So yes, you have my blessing. I wish you would wait a bit, but I also know that there's a war and young people all over the globe are rushing to the registry offices. Is that your intention?"

"We haven't got that far," replied Pia. "I'd rather be married here at Claybourne Court, but don't want the prolonged period of publishing banns and so forth. Isn't there something called a special license?" Pia asked.

"Yes," replied Clay. "I'll speak with the local vicar today. Does your chapel have its own vicar, or do you bring in the gentleman from the village church?"

"The village church. He's very kind and accommodating. I think he's a bit of a romantic. I suspect we can convince him to do our bidding. Especially if he thinks we're going to sacrifice our souls by having a registry office marriage." They all laughed.

"No fancy gown, no bridesmaids, no church filled with flowers?" questioned Lily.

"Perhaps a few flowers, and of course a bouquet. Nothing terribly fussy. Just meaningful words to last a lifetime. I'd like Susie to stand up for me. Clay has a good friend from the camp. Several actually. That will be your choice," she declared, turning to him with a smile.

"I didn't know I got to make a choice. How wonderful."

They continued to talk about their plans, and Lily had Mrs. Briggs bring a bottle of fine champagne. It was against rationing rules, but no one cared. She rounded up Colonel Bradley Barton and asked him if he would like to join them in a toast. The colonel smiled, realizing that the anxieties of only a few days before had dissipated. He too, was impressed when he met the young man in question. Lily also summoned Lady Cynthia from the Dower House. She came graciously, showing none of the former hostility that she'd felt towards Pia. She, too, was charmed by Clay. Her own life had picked up considerably since attending the country house party given by her friend the Duke of Wessex, Aubrey Belmont, early in the summer. Since that time she'd seen a great deal of him. Lily suspected that a wedding announcement from her wasn't out of the question.

Everyone drank to Pia and Clay's happiness, and Lily's misgivings receded into the distance.

⌘

On June 15, 1940, at ten o'clock in the morning, Pia Sabina Claybourne married Clayton Woolridge Marshall in the lovely chapel at Claybourne Court. She wore a simple long-sleeved day dress in crème silk, with a sweet hat, sporting a pretty veil. She held to her vow, having nothing fancy, but it was an enchanting wedding none-the-less. Clay wore his handsome RAF blue dress uniform, and his close friend, Squadron Leader Hugh Danvers, acted as best man. Susie Gatewood stood next to Pia, holding an exquisite bouquet that was a combination of pink roses, peonies, white violets, and lilies. Susie also wore a simple dress in pale, pink silk. There was only family present, and not even all of them. Win found it impossible to procure a leave since he'd been off during his recuperation from Dunkirk. Of course Jordan was there, drinking in every detail since it was his first wedding. He was fifteen years old and a student at Eton. Events like weddings were starting to have interest for him. He was even more taken by Clay's RAF uniform. He was adamant that if the war lasted until he was eighteen, he'd join the RAF. Lily didn't argue with him, but naturally she hoped that all of the horror would be over by then. In any event, she would never have allowed him to stop his education. He would be going on to Oxford at eighteen.

Also present were John and Gena Garrett, Elisabeth and Will Morris, their son David with his wife Jane and daughter Melinda. Lady Cynthia sat proudly in the family pew. Pia wanted the entire staff at Claybourne Court to be present, and so they were. Clay's parents were both deceased, and he was an only child, so there was no representative from his family. He did have an elderly Uncle in Cornwall, but it was difficult for him to travel, and he wasn't able to be there. Colonel Brad Barton came too, at Lily's request, since he had been the one to whom she had shared her concerns about the budding romance. There had been general consternation in the Great House when the announcement was made that Pia was to be married in such a short time. But after everyone met Clay Marshall, they were duly impressed and certain that Pia had made a wise decision. It was abundantly clear that the couple was very much in love. Lily felt tears in her eyes when Pia walked to the altar on Clay's arm. Her memories immediately skipped to that cold day in November, when Pia had appeared on the doorstep at Claybourne Court at age sixteen. What a long journey they had taken since then. Lily knew that Kit would have been so proud of his daughter, at everything she had accomplished in her short life, and at her choice of the man she was meant to spend the remainder of it with. Kit would have described Clay as a "man's man", which was the highest compliment he ever gave to male counterparts, including John Garrett.

After the ceremony, everyone returned to Claybourne Court where a wedding breakfast was held. Clay only had the weekend off before returning to RAF Filton. The Germans had already begun their bombing of targets in England, in an attempt to force a surrender. Everyone knew that although London had escaped the Luftwaffe up until then, it was only a matter of time before they sent their ghastly planes to try to destroy the capital city. It would be a brutal fight and every RAF member would be needed.

Thus, there was no time for a wedding trip. In fact there would be only two nights. Lady Cynthia said that she would move out of the Dower House and into the Great House so that the young couple could spend their first two nights of married life in private. Clay would leave early on Monday morning. The cook, butler and other kitchen help would stay on to attend to their needs. Pia had been so grateful to Lady Cynthia, and if there had been difficulties between them in years past, they were all forgotten and forgiven. It was the nicest gift that her grandmother might have given to Pia. So when the breakfast ended, there was a little mingling and lots of hugs and kisses, but then Pia and Clay disappeared down the flagstone path to the Dower House. Once the door was closed, they weren't seen again, although they were spotted once on Sunday afternoon strolling in the garden. Otherwise, all was quiet.

Very early on Monday morning, June 17, 1940, Pia and Clay emerged from the Dower House. Clay was in uniform, ready to return to his station and join his fellow RAF chaps in the battle he knew was coming. Pia darted into the Great House to announce that they were leaving. She was driving him back to RAF Filton and then returning to London where she intended to announce her marriage to the studio, and try to negotiate her way out of the time remaining on her contract. Whatever the outcome, she would be returning to Claybourne Court that night, since the studio was closed. Everyone spilled out of the house and shook Clay's hand, wishing him good luck and godspeed. It hadn't taken long for all of them to become very fond of him, and it was hard to see him go.

When Pia arrived back home at about seven o'clock, she looked tired and a bit sad. Naturally it was difficult to say goodbye to one's husband less than forty-eight hours after vows were exchanged. Lily doubted that she'd had much sleep during their short time in the Dower House. Pia smiled anemically at Lily and said that she couldn't get out of her contract. That was the primary thing causing her long face. The studio was furious that she'd run off and married with no forewarning. They had to move quickly to put out a press release announcing to the world that she was now Pia Marshall. Though she would not be changing her name professionally, the public would be hungry for every detail about the man who had finally won her heart. There was more angst because she hadn't provided a photo of the groom. Intrepid reporters were able to find several pictures of Clay in various poses by his Hurricane airplane, and one taken upon graduation from the flying training school. Pia didn't have any idea when she would have to uphold the portion of her contract that bound her to two more full-length films. The writers were still at work, in the belief that the theaters would soon open, as the public began to clamor for some sort of entertainment. There was no question that whatever films were slated would focus on the drama of wartime.

Pia wasn't the sort to ruminate over things she couldn't change, so she sighed and said that she intended to go along with her life, and do what she had to do when the time came. Then she disappeared up the stairway to her old room with a stack of stationery, ready to post letters to her husband every day.

11

From July until September the Luftwaffe began its strategy of trying to extinguish Britain's air power by targeting industrial cities, RAF airfields, ports and support cities. However, their plans weren't successful. Hitler was infuriated by the fact that the Nazis couldn't seem to achieve the results they wanted and decided to switch tactics. At first they bombed during daylight hours, but then switched to night time in an attempt to minimize their losses. While some damage was sustained, they found that the RAF was simply superior. The Germans believed that their decision to target London with a massive bombing attack would force the British into a battle of total destruction, and surrender. On the afternoon of September 5, 1940, German bombers appeared in the skies over London. At around four o'clock in the afternoon, 348 German bombers, escorted by 631 fighters, blasted London until six o'clock in the evening.

Two hours later, guided by the fires set by the first assault, a second group of raiders began another attack that lasted until four thirty the following morning. It was the beginning of the Blitz, a period of concentrated bombing and airborne raids. For the next fifty-seven consecutive days, London was bombed either during the day or night. Fires raged in many parts of the city. Residents searched for shelter wherever they could find it. Many bolted to underground shelters that protected as many as 177,000 people during the night. In one episode alone, 450 were killed when a bomb demolished a school.

Clay Marshall spent more time in his Hurricane than he did on the ground. All of the pilots began to call their planes "the office". Naturally Pia was frantic. Had she been able to see the streets of London, she would have been beside herself. Children sat on the ground, amidst the rubble of their homes, and shattered glass covered streets and sidewalks. Block after block of houses were demolished, particularly in the East End of the city. Air-raid sirens could be heard throughout the night, summoning citizens to shelter. Many went to their cellars and were trapped when houses fell on top of them. Fires lined the horizon, bringing a hateful sort of beauty along the banks of the Thames. The people of London were incredibly courageous. They straightened their backs and swept the rubble away, waiting for the next raid with firm resolve. A blackout was in effect all night, every night. Lily received word from Maddie Brooks Pettigrove, her V.A.D. chum, that their dear friend Poppy was killed when her house collapsed upon her. Memories of her smiling face and inspiring strength during the Great War were overwhelming. Lily wished with all of her heart that both Poppy and Maddie had heeded her warning and come to her at Claybourne Court where they would have been safe. But, just as in 1916, Poppy's primary concern had been the care of others, and this time she'd given her life because of her generous spirit. Maddie chose to remain in London. She was working for the Red Cross and they needed every volunteer they could get, especially ones with valid nursing credentials. Her husband, who was in his forties, was a newspaper executive who had done his part in the Great War. Lily had met him and thought he was a dear chap. They'd had no children, primarily because of the war, Lily suspected.

There was pain in the hearts of every British person, but little could be done. It was the RAF's fight and they were heroes of the sky. It was those brave men to whom Winston Churchill referred in his August 21, 1940, speech when he said, "Never in the field of human conflict was so much owed by so many to so few." Pia's beloved husband Clay was one of the pilots who was flying sorties over Germany, facing unimaginable danger.

Clay and Pia saw very little of each other during that time. When Clay had a chance, he scribbled notes to her, and she continued to write daily letters. Occasionally he rang her, but she would burst into tears at the sound of his voice, so there was little conversation. In September she told him that she was expecting a baby. She had fallen into the "pudding club" during their two nights in the Dower House, and although not planned, they were very happy. Clay said it gave him even stronger determination to see the horror through, and Pia believed it was meant to be. If the absolute worst came to pass, she would always have a part of him with her. The baby was due in March, and Pia was in excellent health. With her stepmother as her physician she felt secure, knowing she'd have the best care. Once again, her film studio was infuriated at the news. It meant no film could begin until after the baby was born. Pia told them to write a script that called for a pregnant woman. Although she was joking, that's exactly what was done. A story about an ordinary British family during wartime was developed, and Pia began filming in November of 1940 at Twickenham Studios in London.

Lily wasn't pleased about the location of the set for Pia's new film. The studio was some ten miles from the center of London, but no one could predict where and when the Luftwaffe would drop their gruesome bombs. Pia was five months pregnant when filming began, but the schedule called for three more months of work. That brought her very close to the actual due date of the baby in March. Lily made plans to take leave from her practice and accompany Pia to London for the last month of filming.

Clay caught a break over the holidays and returned to Claybourne Court to be with his wife and her family over Christmas. Win was also home. Upon his arrival, he and Susie announced that they were going to marry while he had a leave from the army. Lily wasn't surprised as they had certainly waited long enough. Of course, Jordan was home from Eton, begging his mother to allow him to quit and join the RAF. He wasn't even sixteen yet, so Lily wasn't concerned. The boy followed Clay around like a puppy, asking question after question about what it was like to fight the Nazis. Clay advised him to stay in school and get all of the education possible before he joined up. His advice put the matter to rest.

Almost all of the patients who'd been billeted at Claybourne Court were discharged. If at all possible they were allowed to return to their homes for the holiday season. The only ones remaining were those who had lost limbs or eyesight and had a need for longer-term recuperation. There were also some men suffering from shell-shock, who occupied private rooms on the third level. Lily made certain that there was a festive atmosphere for those left behind, and of course their families were more than welcome to visit, either for Christmas day or for an overnight. Colonel Brad Barton had become a familiar fixture at Claybourne Court, and Lily sometimes thought about what it would be like when he moved on to other duties and the house was once again a typical English country estate. She'd grown fonder of him than she wanted to admit and suspected that he felt the same about her. There had been no words to that effect, nor any untoward gestures, but they enjoyed many long chats and got on awfully well. If she was in love with him, it wasn't the fiery passion she'd felt for Kit. She knew that could never come again. But, it was a comfortable companionship, combined with a physical attraction that she couldn't deny. He was a handsome man, one she knew a person could lean on. He made her feel secure and cared for. For so many years, Lily had held the reins and pulled the family along, saving them from bankruptcy and disgrace. With the new military contract for uniform fabric, the Claybourne Mill was very successful. That, in turn, contributed to a healthy economy in Claybourne-on-Colne. It was a nice feeling to know that a handsome, kind military man was there to share her burdens. Whether she was ready for anything other than friendship was a vexing question. The thought of going through learning to live with another person was enough to make Lily believe that she would be better to leave her life as it was, not terribly filled with passion, but abundantly blessed with the love of family and friends. She wondered if perhaps Brad felt the same way.

Lady Cynthia had a visitor over the Christmas holidays. Lord Aubrey Belmont wrote and asked if he might be welcome to spend the week between Christmas and the New Year at Claybourne Court. It was apparent to Lily that a bit more than the revival of an old friendship was taking place. Of course, the invitation was immediately sent, and the refined gentleman arrived on Christmas Eve. He was assigned a room in the family wing in the Great House, but spent the majority of his time with Lady Cynthia at the Dower House. They both joined the entire family for Christmas festivities and for the lovely dinner that Mary prepared, in spite of rationing.

On the day following Christmas, Boxing Day, Win and Susie married in the Claybourne Court chapel. There hadn't been time for a lot of fuss, and they didn't want it. Fuss didn't seem appropriate when the war was consuming so much of their energy. Susie wore a simple crème woolen suit with a sweet matching hat, and Win was attired in his army dress uniform. Lily couldn't help imagining what it would have been like had Kit been there. She shed a tear when she thought of his deep love for Win, and of how proud he would be of his son. Then she smiled when she thought about how the bride and groom had met, while throwing stones in a stream when they were small children. It was the first time a Countess of Gloucester had grown up in one of the tenant houses on the estate. How the world had changed.

On New Year's Eve everyone in the family gathered to welcome 1941. There wasn't a lot of joy, as fear about what lay ahead overshadowed the usual celebratory nature of the night. Instead of shouts of happiness at midnight, a solemn prayer was said for God to watch over their beleaguered land. A breakfast was served at one o'clock in the morning, and everyone tried to perk up a bit while enjoying Mary's usual delicious offerings. As they sat in the dining hall, enjoying tea, coffee, and an occasional glass of Port, Lord Belmont stood and tapped the rim of his glass.

All heads turned, and there was silence in the room.

"I have an announcement to make," he began. "Lady Cynthia and I have made the decision to marry. Obviously we're past the age where we expect the fuss that these young people deserve when they're just beginning life, but we have both lived enough years to know that we want to spend the remainder of the time we have left with each other. I'd like you all to join in our happiness. I shall treasure her until the day I leave this earth."

When he sat down everyone burst into applause. There was genuine pleasure at witnessing two people who'd both been loved before, step forward and announce that they were ready to form a new and lasting chapter to their stories. Everyone stood, and an impromptu queue was formed. Everyone clasped their hands and kissed cheeks, wishing them long lives filled with everlasting love. When asked when they intended to marry, they replied that it would be soon, but that they wanted it to be very private, just the two of them. The family understood. They wished to share the sacred moment with only each other, and no one objected. Their marriage would mean a change for Lily. The Dower House would be empty, and that would allow her to move her belongings to the smaller, quaint home. Susie would have sole charge of Claybourne Court, yet Lily would be nearby to help her. The house would keep its furnishings, but for a few items Lady Cynthia wished to take with her to Belmont Hall, so the move wouldn't entail too much difficulty.

So, the short period of respite from the war ended, and the military men went back to duty. Clay was assigned to a new station, RAF Fowlmere. Win continued to move about in both England and Scotland, learning new tactical measures in the event that the British Expeditionary Forces became engaged with the enemy, which was virtually an inescapable conclusion. While no one knew about it at that point in time, the allies had plans underway to open another front in the war. Operation Overlord was the code name, and extensive preparations were underway for an amphibious landing in France. Practice runs were being done at various beaches and newly designed equipment was being tested.

In February, 1941, Lily accompanied Pia to the set at Twickenham, where the last filming was wrapping up. Pia was in fine shape, eight months pregnant, but not terribly large and as lovely as ever. Her fans had embraced her marriage with enormous love. Cards and parcels arrived daily at Claybourne Court, and at the studio, meant for the baby's arrival. Clay hadn't been home since Christmas, and Pia knew that he was in the thick of fighting for air supremacy over London and its environs. The area where Twickenham was located had escaped any damage thus far and, of course, Lily and Pia prayed fervently that it would be left untouched.

One of the last scenes in the film was to be shot in a typical Victorian house with three stories and bowed windows. It was supposed to have been set in Nottingham, but was, in reality, near the studio lot where filming was taking place. Instead of using a false front, they had commandeered a genuine home whose owners sold to the studios and evacuated to the country. In the scene being filmed, Pia was a British housewife expecting her first child while her husband was away fighting the war. It was not a difficult role for Pia to play. As the scene got underway, Lily took a chair in the corner of the kitchen, where the cameras wouldn't see her. Pia set about washing dishes and listening to the wireless, while the sound of airplane engines could be heard from above. Suddenly the sirens began to wail, and Pia looked up, startled. This was not written into the script. There were shouts from the cameramen and the director yelled for everyone to seek cover. Pia couldn't run quickly because of her pregnancy, so trying to get to the Anderson shelter across the road didn't seem feasible. Lily grabbed her arm.

"Quickly, Pia. The cellar is our best chance," she cried. There was a doorway from the kitchen with stairs to the cellar, and Pia grabbed the handle, pulling it open. Mother and daughter hurried down the stairway into the dark, damp area below. There were no lights, and it was very hard to see where they were. They felt along the stone walls until they came to a recessed area that seemed to offer better protection. There were bits and pieces of old furniture and a mattress on the floor. Lily pulled it over to the place they planned to shelter. She told Pia to cover herself with the mattress, especially her abdomen, to shield the baby from harm. Then, Lily scrunched underneath too. They lay flat on the cold, stone floor and listened as the planes grew louder and louder.

"Oh my God, Lily. What if they drop their bloody bombs on this house? We'll be killed. Clay will never know his child." Pia was sobbing, and Lily held her hand, doing her best to calm her.

"Shhhh, Pia. We'll get through this. Remember, you're the girl who walked from Rome to England. A few German planes aren't going to do you in."

Pia tried to laugh, but it was clear that she was terrified. So was Lily. There was an enormous crash, and the entire house shook. The first din was followed by a second. The worst had happened. The sound was horrendous, as chandeliers dropped to the floor and walls began to collapse. They tucked their heads under the mattress and began to pray. They could feel large items hurtling down around them, and something massive collapsed directly on top of the mattress. In spite of the protection it yielded, both Lily and Pia felt pain when whatever had fallen came to rest upon them. They lay together in silence, waiting to see what else would happen. They could hear planes fading away in the distance. Debris kept falling in sporadic masses from above. Lily finally moved her head enough so that she could look up at what had been the ceiling. There was nothing but open sky now. By slowly moving, inch by inch, she was finally able to determine what had fallen upon them. It appeared that they were hopelessly pinned beneath a huge beam that must have held part of the roof. She thought for a moment before she spoke to Pia. She saw no need to upset her further by telling her that it looked as if they were not about to get out on their own. Lily was frantic herself, but her primary concern was her daughter and the baby. Finally, Pia's voice came from beside her.

"Lily, how are we going to get out? I'm frightened."

Lily decided she had to be honest. Pia was a bright, sensible girl, and if there was ever a time when two heads were better than one, this was it. She might be able to suggest something that Lily hadn't thought of.

"Pia. Please try to stay calm, for the sake of the baby, sweetheart. I fear we're in quite a muddle here. I can see what looks like a beam or girder. It's lying directly on top of us. If we hadn't crawled beneath the mattress, I'm afraid that would have been the end. But I don't see a way that we can get out from under this bloody thing. Can you think of anything we might do? The house is in shambles. When I look up, all I see is sky. Obviously, the roof is gone."

"Oh God, Lily, no. But, surely the film people will know that we're missing. As soon as the all-clear sounds, don't you think they'll come searching for us?"

"Yes. Of course," answered Lily. "That is, if they made it to the Anderson shelter. It appeared to be such a short time between the sirens and the explosion. Maybe it only seemed like that to us."

"Lily, are you hurt anywhere? If I go into labor, I'll need you to be able to help me. Do you think you could?"

"I don't think I'm hurt. Probably some scratches and such. I don't feel anything dreadful. But, Pia why are you talking about labor? You're a month away from your due date yet," Lily said, in an alarmed voice.

"Because I feel like I'm having some cramping. It couldn't be the baby, could it?"

"It may be just the trauma of this whole ordeal. Try to take deep breaths, and remain calm. Someone will come to rescue us. I'm afraid if we try to squirm out from under here, that beam thing is likely to crash right onto our bodies."

There was silence, and Lily could hear Pia taking deep breaths. Lily flexed her fingers and tried to move her arms. If Pia needed her, she was damned well going to be there for her.

12

"Oh God, Lily! I hear the sound of airplanes again. They aren't back, are they?" Pia cried.

"I don't know, Pia. It could be our men, the RAF. Perhaps Clay is up there right now, making certain that we're protected."

"Oh, I do hope so. But Lily, the vibration of their engines could cause a shifting of this mammoth mess that's hanging precariously over us. Pray that they don't fly any lower."

They could hear no more sirens wailing, which seemed to bode well for the fact that it must not be the Luftwaffe. They lay in silence for a bit longer.

"Pia, how is your cramping?" Lily asked.

"I didn't want to worry you, but it hasn't gone away. In fact, it's grown more pronounced."

"More pronounced. In what way?"

"Stronger. More painful," Pia answered.

"Are the cramps coming any more frequently?" Lily could feel her heart speed up.

"I can't be certain. If so, not by very much," Pia answered.

"Keep lying still, and breathe slowly and calmly. I'm going to try to move very, very slowly so that I'm positioned at your feet. If it should come to the worst, I want to try to be in a place to help you."

"Oh God, Lily. Be careful. The wrong move could bring this whole thing down upon us. Its full weight isn't bearing on us now."

"I know. I'll be careful. But our only hope is for me to be in a position to deliver the baby if it comes to that. Don't get too alarmed yet. It may not happen. But it's better to be safe and ready. While I'm trying to inch over into position, I want you to be thinking of anything at hand that could be used, especially something to tie off a baby's cord. These certainly aren't the most sterile conditions, but I imagine babies have had worse starts in life."

"Lily, I'm so glad I have you here. I would simply lay here and die without you."

"No, no you wouldn't, Pia. You're strong and brave, and you'd do whatever has to be done to save your baby. For now just remain still, but follow any directions I give you, and tell me if your pains are worse or closer together."

"All right," Pia answered, plaintively.

Before Lily began to move, she glanced up and down to see if she could spot anything that might be of use in the delivery of a baby. The mattress presented some possibilities. Lily knew that if a premature baby was delivered in such conditions, it would need warmth. The cellar was cold, and she would need something in which to wrap the newborn child. The mattress offered the best hope. She reached up and felt about. It was definitely covered by a protective pad, but also, as her fingers kept exploring, she realized that at one end there was a curled up, old blanket. She felt like it was manna from heaven. Now the most essential thing was for her to be in a position to help Pia, and Pia needed to be able to move her legs. All of this seemed impossible, given the circumstances. She slowly inched her way around until, after perhaps an hour, she was facing Pia's legs. Before the two of them had been lying side by side. Now they were facing one another. Lily had accomplished one important step. Still, unless Pia could move her legs, it would all be for naught. The cramps seemed to have intensified a bit, but Lily wasn't too worried about time. This was a first baby, and that was on their side.

"Pia dear, now I need you to help me. You've got to be able to move your legs if a delivery becomes necessary. I want you to try flexing your toes, to make sure you can feel them and to get circulation going. Then, very, very slowly see if you can raise your knees up. We're in a good air pocket under here. You can see where the mattress is folded upward, almost into a tent-like position in the middle. That not only gives us some room to maneuver, but also helps with breathing."

Pia began to bring her legs up, ever so slowly. At one point she stopped when she heard the sound of something shifting. It was the girder and whatever else rested on top of it. For all they knew, it could be portions of the roof or wooden beams. When the shifting occurred, Pia froze like a frightened rabbit, and so did Lily. Waiting several minutes, she tried again. Her movements were nearly imperceptible, but she *was* making a bit of progress. Because of the space created by the tented mattress, there was enough room for her to move into the necessary position. Space wasn't the difficulty. The problem was the massive chunks and slabs that rested on top of the beam or girder. If they began to slide and shift position, the force of what Lily believed was a large girder would fall down upon them. Mattress or no mattress, it was hard to think that they would survive, at least not without serious injury. There was the strong smell of cordite in the air, as a result of the wretched bomb, and if Lily moved her head outside of the protected air pocket, it was nearly impossible to see because of the swirling dust from plaster and other building materials.

As Pia continued to bring her legs up, they heard the all clear sound, which meant that if the others on the film set had run to the Anderson shelter, they would be emerging. They would realize that Pia and Lily were missing, if they hadn't already. The logical conclusion would be that they had run to the cellar. Lily hated to think what the house looked like from the outside. It must have been one immense pile of rubble. With the roof gone, and the fact that Lily was able to see the sky, all of the ceilings must have collapsed into the cellar when the roof was destroyed. That was probably responsible for the massive amount of dust in the air. Lily tried to keep her ears tuned to see if she heard any voices from the outside. There was nothing so far. After what seemed an interminable length of time, Pia managed to move her legs to the necessary position. Now they would wait. It was a question of what came first, the baby or the rescue squad.

In only a few moments they could hear the voices of men calling their names.

"Oh, thank God, Lily. We'll be saved," Pia cried.

"Yes, dear, let's hope so," Lily replied. While the sound of voices was a joy, Lily knew that it wouldn't be a simple rescue. They couldn't easily reach down and pluck them out. The whole mess was tilting tenuously. Some system would have to be derived, and it could take hours. Still, it was reassuring to think that someone knew where they were.

"Lily! Pia! Where are you? Can you hear us? Lily? Lily? Pia? Answer, if you can hear us," the men shouted.

At first they were too frightened to answer. What if the sound of their voices caused something to fall? Finally Lily decided that they had to let the men know that they were trapped. She would have to chance it.

"This is Lily Claybourne. I'm down here with Pia. We're trapped in the cellar," she shouted. Nothing moved, and she became braver. "Can you hear us?" she screamed.

"Yes, we can hear you, Lily. Are you injured? Is Pia's baby all right?"

"Yes, so far. But, we're completely trapped under a large piece of debris, both a girder and a beam with more debris on top of that, perhaps furniture, perhaps parts of walls or the roof. I'm afraid if we try to get out, we'll cause everything to crash upon us. We're under a mattress now, and have an air pocket. Pia is having some pains that could be the beginning of labor."

There was silence. "Can you still hear me?" she shouted.

"Yes, we hear you. You're in quite a pickle, aren't you? First things first. If it became necessary, could you deliver a baby down there?" shouted one of the men.

"Yes. I think so. It obviously wouldn't be ideal, but I'd do my best," answered Lily.

"Do you think it's possible for us to drop any necessary items down to you? If we could clear a small space, we might be able to attach a rope to a basket and send down anything you need."

"It would be a godsend," Lily answered, "but only if you were able to position a clearing so that it dropped directly above us. Obviously, neither of us can scamper about the cellar, retrieving a basket."

"We would have to drop a rope first, and get it positioned correctly, with precise measurements. If we can do this, what would be your most essential needs?"

"A warm baby blanket, towels, forceps just in case, a pair of sterile scissors, a role of bandage, a small scalpel, wet flannel cloths. Naturally, I'd like some painkiller, but that isn't strictly necessary. Only if for some unknown reason I had to perform a Caesarean. Any of those items would be better than nothing," Lily answered.

"What about water?"

"Water would be terrific, a godsend. But, I don't see how you could get it down here?"

"In a large jar or several cans, or bottles. Let us see what we can do. There's a building engineer on his way to sort out what would be the most feasible way to get you out of there. We're making the baby our first concern, and the engineer will work on other aspects."

Lily reached over and patted Pia. "Well dear, this isn't perfect, but at least we have help, and we have to trust that they'll provide what we need."

"Lily, I'm so frightened. I think I may have wet myself."

"Oh my. I don't think so, Pia. I think that's your water breaking. It's a sign that the baby would like to make its entrance into the world."

Lily tried to keep her voice light, but this new wrinkle worried her greatly. She was praying that the rescue party could round up the necessary items she'd requested, and get them to her before it was necessary to use them. Of course the birth could still be a long way off. Pia was putting her hand over her midsection and making whimpering noises.

"Are you hurting dreadfully, Pia?" Lily asked.

"Not dreadfully. But a lot more than in the beginning. This is really it, isn't it Lily? I'm so sorry I got you into this mess. I should have refused to do this film. It was pure lunacy. I should be safe in my bed at Claybourne Court now, or in the hospital. I've put both you and Clay's baby into harm's way."

"Now you stop such talk. Things happen. How could any of us have known that the Nazis would target Twickenham? I suspect they'd done their damage to London proper and just threw in that last bit as a goodbye token on their way back to Germany. I hope our boys got them."

"I hope Clay got them," Pia said firmly.

"In any event, it's no one's fault, except of course the beastly Germans. Don't you dare put the responsibility upon yourself. We live in a dangerous world at the moment, and we're learning how to cope. Just imagine. Won't this be a story to tell your son or daughter?"

Pia tried to laugh. "It will be, won't it?" she answered.

The minutes ticked by. Lily was thankful for the timepiece she always wore on her wrist. It had been about forty-five minutes since the last conversation with their rescuers.

Before long there was the sound of voices again. "Are you ladies still doing all right?" someone shouted.

"Yes. We're holding our own. Pia's pains are increasing somewhat. I'd feel better if we could have those items I called for."

"We have them here. I don't want either of you to be concerned when you hear the noise that'll be created when we begin to clear a space to drop the supplies down. We've taken a good appraisal of the situation, and you need to trust that we know what we're doing."

"May I ask to whom I'm speaking?" Lily asked.

"Yes, Milady. My name is Jonathan Bradstreet. The mates working with me are called Jim, Ian, Nigel, Simon, and Ron. We'll worry about last names later. They're a good bunch. We've all dealt with situations like this before. Try to be calm, and trust that we'll get you out."

"Thank you, Jonathan, and thank the others. Can you do something else for us?"

"If it's possible, we'll certainly try."

Get ahold of anyone you can at our home, Claybourne Court in Claybourne-on-Colne, and tell them what's happened. Make certain that Pia's husband Group Captain Clayton Marshall, RAF, is notified."

"That's already been taken care of. The studio contacted your family immediately. I believe a Colonel Barton is on his way here, as well as Mrs. Marshall's husband."

"That's splendid news," shouted Lily. "All right, go ahead with whatever you have to do. We'll grit our teeth and try to be calm."

Over an hour passed, while the sound of heavy drilling and the scraping of wood could be heard. Pia and Lily closed their eyes and prayed that the vibration wouldn't cause more shifting of debris. At long last, the noise came to an end.

"All right, Dr. Claybourne. We think we have a space sufficient to lower a basket large enough to carry the items you requested. We've tried to gauge exactly where it will be lowered, and expect that it will come in directly over you. We'll lower it all the way to the floor, so don't interrupt its motion when it enters your eyesight. Take out the items you need, and leave the basket there. After the baby has been safely delivered, wrap it in the blanket, and place it in the basket. Then let us know it's in there. We'll bring the little rascal up to the surface. Then we'll begin working on getting you out of there."

"Thank you so much. I feel better with some implements to assist me. Pia's a strong girl. We're going to get this done."

Night had fallen by the time Pia's pains were sufficiently close together, and she was ready to bring her baby into the world. She was amazingly resilient. Lily remembered when she had assisted in delivering Eleanor's baby back in 1915 and the way she had carried on. Pia was stoic and only whimpered occasionally when the pain became unbearable. Lily told her to go ahead and scream, but Pia said that everyone who was helping them would be more concerned if they heard her making a fuss. Instead, Lily gave her a towel. She pulled on it and bit down with her teeth. At 9: 47 p.m., Pia was delivered of a beautiful baby girl. The men had sent a torch down, and Lily was able to show Pia her lovely baby. The tiny bundle had very dark hair, like her mother, and what looked like beautiful features. She was so small, it was hard to make out too much about her in the dim cellar. Lily cut the cord and wrapped a bandage around it. The little girl was swaddled in the baby blanket, and Lily cleaned her face with a flannel. The men up above could hear her lusty cries. Lily took care of the rest of the delivery, and placed the baby on Pia's chest for a moment. She wanted to get the baby to hospital as quickly as possible, since she was premature and probably in need of an incubator. But she knew that Pia would have been beside herself if she couldn't at least have held her daughter. Lily asked what she and Clay were going to name her.

"Originally we'd planned on Mary Lily, after our two mothers. But with all that's happened tonight, I believe I'll call her Brittan because she was born at a time when our country was fighting for her life. But we'll spell it B-r-i-t-t-a-n. I like that better. Clay and I will talk about second names later."

"Oh Pia, I think that's lovely, "Lily responded. "What a pretty name for a special baby." Lily placed her in the basket and called out to the men above. "One little girl, coming up. Her name is Brittan Marshall," Lily laughed as the baby let out a lusty wail.

13

Brittan was rushed to St. Bart's Hospital and placed into an incubator. Though she was a month early, her lungs appeared to be fully developed, and she passed all tests with flying colors.

Back at the collapsed house, the rescue mission moved into phase two. By then both Clay Marshall and Brad Barton were there. Clay had time to see his daughter and was delighted with her, but he made the decision to stay with his wife rather than travel to the hospital. He would not feel completely at ease until he knew that Pia was safe.

The engineer went to work. The next part of the job would be much more difficult.

The idea was to enlarge the place they had opened to send down medical supplies and to bring the baby back up. Then one man would be lowered into the cellar to inspect the situation and make a recommendation about how best to go about freeing Pia and Lily. Pia had fallen asleep after the ordeal of giving birth, and Lily lay on her back, dozing off and on. At two-o'clock in the morning, Jonathan called down and said that he was going to be lowered. Both Lily and Pia came awake and watched with trepidation as his body was slowly lowered on a steel cable into the debris-filled cellar.

When he reached the bottom he treaded very gently to where Lily and Pia lay, still cocooned under their mattress.

"Thank God you came upon this old thing," Jonathan said. "It's served quite a good purpose tonight."

"Do you see a way to free us from this muddle?" Lily asked.

"I think we're going to have to bring several more men down here and very gingerly remove the debris that's lying on the girder and beam. Then we're going to have to lift both of those off you, so that you can free yourself from their weight. You'll have to move quickly because there's a lot of weight, and even with several men, it will be hard to hold it for too long."

"We'll scurry like rats in the night," answered Pia.

"Then we'll be in business," Jonathan laughed. "Are you in any pain, Pia? Will that make it harder for you to move?"

"Not significantly. I can do it. Just get the bloody thing off me."

Jonathan laughed. "Oh, if your fans could hear you now," he chuckled.

"I don't bloody care," she retorted.

He was lifted back up, as he hung onto the sturdy cable. He had a meeting with the others involved, and all were in agreement with his plan. One by one, men were lowered into the cellar. Two men were left above to hoist them back up on the return trip. Clay and Brad were there, but they didn't come down into the cellar. They weren't trained for that sort of rescue and were also considered too emotional. Once all of the men were in place, they began to carefully lift off the pieces of rubble piled high on the top of the girder and beam. Slowly but surely they made progress until they were down to only the last remaining barriers.

"All right, ladies. This is the end game. Let us explain exactly how it will work. All but one of us will lift the beam, and move it to the floor. This has to be done very carefully so that the girder doesn't shift position and crash further down. When we've got that off of you, we'll lift the girder. The thing must weigh a ton. Once we get it into the air, the two of you need to be ready to slip out from under and clear yourself from the area. Make certain you get as far as you can from this spot. After you're out, we'll let it crash back onto the mattress. Then we'll start hoisting you to the ground level. Do you understand?"

"Yes, perfectly," Lily answered. She was terrified, but tried not to let it show in her voice. If a mistake was made, and they didn't get out as planned, the girder could crash back down with full force on one or both of them. Both she and Pia took deep breaths and waited. After moving the beam to the floor, three men positioned themselves at each end of the mammoth piece of girder, and began to use all of their strength to lift it. As soon as they gave the word, Pia and Lily slithered out from under the mattress and ran as fast as they could to the opposite corner of the cellar. Their legs were stiff and, for a moment, they weren't certain they were going to be able to pull it off, but they ignored the numbness in their limbs and stumbled away from the ghastly spot where they had lain for hours. As soon as it was clear that they were both safely away from what could have been their grave, the men tried to slowly lower the girder. At the very last moment it slipped from one hand and crashed to the ground. Everyone jumped back and sighed in relief. They had accomplished what they'd set out to do.

Everyone was silent for a few moments while they regained their bearings and silently thanked God for the safe rescue they had completed. Then, Pia and Lily were shown how to grip the steel cable and hold themselves securely while lifted upward. When Pia arrived at the surface first, her husband was waiting to take her into his arms. She simply dropped from the cable into his embrace.

"Oh my God, Pia. I thought I was going to lose you. You and our baby. I can't believe this has turned out so well," Clay murmured, holding her close to his chest and kissing her on the neck.

"Just be thankful that Lily was with me, Clay. If it hadn't been for her, we wouldn't have our baby. She acted as skillfully as she might have in an operating room."

"I am thankful, Pia. This has been the longest night of my life. I can't imagine what you've been through."

"I think I fared quite well, considering," she smiled. "Once I knew the baby was all right, I rather knew that we were in safe hands and would come out of it fine."

Clay rolled his eyes. "These chaps who rescued you are one incredible group of men. We owe them so much," he said.

At that moment Lily arrived in their midst. Brad Barton ran over to her side and held out his arms. "My God, Lily. This was a nightmare," he nearly sobbed, in a trembling voice. Lily put her head on his shoulder and allowed him to hold her. "Thank you for coming, Brad. It means a lot to have someone hold me after such an ordeal," she murmured.

"I was frantic with worry. The moment the call came, I jumped into the car. I can't imagine what I'd have done if you'd been killed. This made me realize what a huge part of my life you've become."

"And you've become exceedingly important to me, Brad," she echoed. Nothing more was said, but it was obvious that they had moved a step closer to expressing some long held feelings.

The entire group was placed into a waiting auto and taken to the same hospital where baby Brittan lay in a warm incubator. Pia, Lily, Clay, and Brad insisted upon visiting the nursery before allowing the medical staff to do an examination on the two women. The baby was laying on her side, sucking her tiny thumb. She had a mass of dark hair and Pia's coloring. Her eyes were Clay's, a sapphire blue. She was a little over four pounds, but everything was perfect. She would just need to gain some weight before she could be taken home. Pia and Clay were allowed to put on sterile gowns and hold their little girl for a few minutes. They both had tears streaming down their faces. They made a perfect family.

After the visit to the nursery, Pia and Lily were taken to the casualty area where they underwent thorough examinations. Both of them were given a perfect bill of health and didn't even need so much as a bandage. The decision was made for them to stay overnight, simply as a precautionary measure, and both Clay and Brad insisted upon staying with them. They were assigned side-by-side private rooms. Finally the end to a harrowing night came, as the sun began to rise above the pitifully damaged city.

The Blitz continued until May 21, 1941. By that time everyone was safely back at Claybourne Court, except for Group Captain Clay Marshall, who rejoined the fight after a scant two days of leave. Brittan was ensconced in the nursery, and she was most definitely the highlight of Pia's life. Pia refused to return to complete the film they'd been in the midst of when the attack came, nor would she consider returning to conclude the last film on her contract. She told the studio they could sue her, but that nothing on God's green earth would make her return. Naturally the studio head wasn't a fool, and knew that the publicity following a lawsuit would be untenable. To try and force his top actress to return to a place where she had almost lost her life, and the life of her first child, would be unconscionable. So, while there was a lot of letter writing back and forth, and threats made by the legal office, Pia stood firm. Eventually it was all dropped. She made it abundantly clear that she was finished with acting and intended to devote the rest of her life to being a wife and mother. If Lily had ever worried about the abruptness of Pia's decision to marry Clay, followed by her unexpected honeymoon pregnancy, there was no doubt whatsoever that Pia had known what she was doing. The love between Clay and Pia was very real and obviously filled with commitment.

While the hideous ordeal in London had been taking place, Lady Cynthia and Lord Belmont had surreptitiously sneaked off to his home, Belmont Hall, and married. Lily sent masses of roses and rang to wish her great happiness. There was a promise to celebrate Christmas together. Lady Cynthia was anxious to meet her first great-grandchild. With her mother-in-law settled at Belmont Hall, Lily set about moving to the Dower House. Lady Cynthia had taken everything she wished out of the dwelling, but much of the furniture was left intact. Lily had always loved the house and was thrilled to be making it her own. Susie Claybourne would now have full reign at Claybourne Court, as its new countess. Of course, it was still being utilized as a recuperative hospital and probably would be until the end of the war. Since there had been no battles of great significance on land, the Great House wasn't filled to capacity with military wounded. There *were* RAF cases, men who were wounded when shot down and rescued in the English Channel. Pia sometimes wished that Clay would receive some minor wound and be brought home to recuperate, but she knew that was selfish thinking and never said it aloud.

The summer limped along at Claybourne Court, and the war moved into its third frightful year. Win was home again for two brief weeks, and Susie was filled with joy. The two never left one another's side. Jordan was also there, and he finally received permission from Lily to enlist when he turned eighteen. He promised that he would return to school and go on to Oxford when the war ended. That still meant there were two years of waiting for him, and Lily hoped that there would be no war when he reached the age to join up.

In an attempt to brighten the mood of everyone at Claybourne Court, an outdoor party was planned whereby the families and loved ones of hospital patients could visit, and everyone could have a day outside to enjoy some lovely weather. It wasn't a fancy affair, which would have been impossible anyway, due to rationing and other war restrictions. But Mary made lots of lemonade, and hot tea for those who wanted it, and cold finger sandwiches were piled high on trays. A badminton set was erected in front of the house and the croquet set was assembled in its usual spot on the front lawn. A large tent was erected in case of rain, but it proved to be unnecessary since the day couldn't have been lovelier. Susie and Lily invited friends from the village as well, so there was quite a crowd milling about the grounds.

Emma, the Claybourne nanny from when Win was small, had finally decided to move back with her family, and Pia decided to hire Melinda Morris, David and Jane's daughter, who was now nearing twenty-five to tend to Brittan. Melinda hoped to be able to continue her education and become a teacher, following in the footsteps of her mother, but she didn't want to leave home until the country was at peace again. Melinda adored children so she seemed a natural choice to fill Emma's role. She pushed Brittan about the grounds during the lawn party, and nearly everybody stopped to have a peek at the baby and remark on her beauty. Pia hovered about like an anxious mother hen, but as the day wore on she eased up and circulated among the guests, all of whom knew her fame and wanted to meet her. The lawn was a vivid green, and the trees in full leaf, bent to shade those who relaxed beneath them. All of the roses were blooming, as well as lavender, foxglove, lilacs and lilies. In short, it was a perfect day. Brad Barton strolled about, meeting the families of the patients who were billeted at the Great House, The guests were impressed with his kindness and compassion for the military men who were under his supervision. All of the physicians assigned to the patients were also in attendance, and the families were given the opportunity to ask questions about the condition of their loved ones and learn of their progress. As afternoon fell, people grew drowsy and many drifted off to sleep in the shade of the trees. Children played games and a few hearty souls took each other on in a game of badminton. Melinda parked Brittan's pram beneath a large, old oak tree and settled on the ground beside her. Lily, Pia and Susie continued to visit with guests and trotted back and forth to the house seeing that everything was running smoothly. Over half of the people on the lawn were asleep at one time and even Melinda dozed off against her will. She had been up at the crack of dawn, and the sun had made her unusually sleepy, as it had most everyone else.

When it came time to move the patients back inside and all of the guests began to gather their belongings, there was another flurry of activity as people expressed their gratitude for such a lovely day. So few social events were being held because of the ghastly war footing, so it had been doubly appreciated.

14

Lily felt they had more reason than usual to be thankful that Christmas and made preparations for a nice holiday, allowing Susie to take the lead. There was still no gala planned, as it didn't seem appropriate. The war was by no means over, and England was growing weary. Prime Minister Churchill was a godsend, for just as morale began to plummet, he would give an incredibly inspiring speech and everyone would straighten up and carry on.

Susie and Lily shopped for the family, leaving Pia to enjoy baby Brittan. The only effect on Pia from the ghastly nightmare in the cellar was a total lack of desire to leave home, and most especially to leave Brittan. John and Lily discussed it, and both agreed that it was a normal reaction to such a dreadful fright. It was decided that they wouldn't make an issue out of it, and in time Pia would feel secure enough to emerge from her cocoon. She was more than happy to pitch in with any tasks that needed doing at the Great House, but she balked at leaving the security of home and especially the baby.

On December 7, 1941, the family was sitting in the library listening to the wireless. Lily was knitting a sweater for Brittan and Pia was rocking the baby. Susie was reading a stack of letters from Win that had just arrived. That seemed to be the way it was. One wouldn't receive any mail for an extended period, and then a flood of letters would arrive. Clay wrote to Pia, but also rang her, since he wasn't based a terribly long distance from Claybourne-on-Colne. Lily didn't think it would have mattered if he were. Jordan wasn't home from Eton yet, but was expected on the twentieth. He had finally turned sixteen in September, and Lily dreaded the pleas that would be made once again about leaving school at eighteen and joining the military. That was still two years ahead of them, and she prayed even more fervently that the dreadful war would end by his eighteenth birthday, which would be in the autumn of 1943.

There was a fire roaring in the fireplace, and the house was quiet. All of the patients had settled for an afternoon lie-down, and Brad Barton had just entered the library, asking if he could join them to listen to the news on the wireless. Of course he was made welcome. There was music playing, and all was quiet when an announcer's voice suddenly broke in, saying that the American Navy had suffered a terrible defeat when the Japanese attacked their fleet at Pearl Harbor in the Hawaiian islands. The voice of the president of the United States came over the wireless, announcing that a state of war existed between Japan and the U.S.A. Everyone was stunned. Pia placed Brittan into her cradle, and Lily dropped her knitting. Susie arranged Win's letters into a neat stack and pushed them to the side. It was shocking, terrible news, and yet it also meant a change in their lives because it was what the English had been praying for. Not an attack on America, but the entrance of that powerful country on the Allied side. Everyone started to talk at once with the primary gist of the conversation being the impact on Britain. Brad was the person they turned to for answers, since he was a colonel in the military. He felt quite certain that America would declare war on Germany, and England would have a powerful friend in their fight against the Nazis. They all sat up until the wee hours, listening to news bulletins as they crossed the wires. While they were thrilled to think they were finally going to have help in the dreadful long war, there was genuine heartbreak when they heard of the massive casualties at Pearl Harbor. The poor men had been caught sleeping in their ships on a lovely Sunday morning in what, until then, had been an Eden-like paradise. Scores of ships were sunk, and the station at Hickam Field was heavily bombed. It was hard to imagine what was in the minds of the Japanese. They may have scored a temporary victory, but they had also signed their own death warrants.

⚮

On December 11, Hitler declared war on the United States, and on January 26, the first American soldiers arrived in Great Britain. The tide was about to turn. Clay and Win both wrote of their gratitude for the influx of fresh troops. The Americans were a bit of a cocky bunch, but it was hard to dislike them. Most were quite jolly. Several American nurses arrived at Claybourne Court, and they were a welcome addition to the staff. Lily and Susie enjoyed teaching them English traditions, and in return they learned many new vocabulary words and dances of which they'd never heard. It wasn't long before several of the almost totally recuperated patients were asking the American girls to push them in their wheel chairs on the lawn. Interestingly, it was rumored that the American soldiers thought the English girls exceedingly charming. It was another case of the grass always being greener on the other side.

The war was now in its third year, and although there were more optimistic feelings since the Americans were involved, there still didn't appear to be any definitive end in sight. The British people knew that behind the scenes there had to be a lot of planning taking place, but it was hard not to become war weary. Jordan was only one year away from his eighteenth birthday, and Lily began to realize that unless something major happened before September of 1943, her youngest boy would also be in uniform. He had changed his mind about which branch of the military he wanted to join. For years it had been the RAF, but the more he considered it, the more he thought he might want to try to fight alongside, or at least near, his brother Win. Of course, Win was an officer and Jordan wouldn't be, but his fondest hope was to serve with Win as his commanding officer. So when and if the time came, Jordan had decided he would enlist in the British Expeditionary Forces. Lily still prayed for a miracle and tried to push aside the fact that both of her boys would most probably be fighting.

It seemed like all she could remember was war. From the time she'd been in her early twenties until she was twenty-six, and again from age forty until the present, she'd had all she wanted of war. So had everyone else in

England. They were all weary of marmite sandwiches, four inch baths, blackouts, air-raid sirens and continual anxiety. But they were a strong people, and there was nothing on earth that would have convinced them to surrender to Germany.

The only bright spot that year was when Melinda Morris came to Lily and announced that she was in love with an American airman who was recuperating at Claybourne Court. He had been injured in an air raid over Germany, but had managed to take his damaged plane safely home to his station at RAF Church Fenton. His leg had taken a bullet and it was questionable as to whether he would walk again, but he felt certain that given time and good care he would be joining his mates once again. His name was Sanford St. John, which everyone shortened to Sandy. Though not true members of the RAF, and instead assigned to the American Air Force, the Americans were stationed with the RAF at camps throughout England. He was a pilot, and also a graduate of Duke University. He came from an upper-class family in the southern United States, and Melinda worried that they might not accept her since she certainly wasn't of the aristocracy in Britain. While being the daughter of a chemist was middle-class, she'd been brought up in a modest manner and knew little about the lifestyle of a wealthy American family. Sandy didn't seem at all concerned, but sometimes she wondered. He didn't speak often of his family, and it had never been suggested that someday she would meet them. While he told her he loved her, he never spoke of marriage. In England, the more usual path was that conversation about marriage followed declaration of love. Melinda had high morals and was a proper English girl. She'd always saved herself for a husband, but Sandy swept her off her feet, and she lost her footing with him one day as they walked slowly across the lawns exercising his leg. She wasn't sorry it had happened, as she truly loved him, but she was frightfully anxious, waiting for him to say something about the future. Her strict moral upbringing had taught her that men were the ones who did the proposing.

She went to Lily and told the truth about everything. Lily was not at all critical, but was deeply concerned that Sandy St. John might be playing Melinda for a fool. All of the young, unmarried women had been warned to be wary of American men, as not all could be trusted to be honest when it came to affairs of the heart. Lily even considered speaking with the airman in private, but it didn't seem her place to do so. She wondered about telling David and Jane Morris, but Melinda was not a child. She was, in fact, going on twenty-five years old. Although she seemed much younger, in her country-girl innocence, Lily was certain Melinda would have been embarrassed and chagrined if her parents interfered. So the best Lily could accomplish was to warn her about unscrupulous men, without making it sound as if she didn't trust Melinda to know her own feelings. More importantly, she didn't want Sandy St. John to be trifling with sweet Melinda. Lily did plead with her not to engage in any more lovemaking, but once the line had been crossed, it was unlikely that things would reverse themselves, of which Lily was well aware.

Lily liked Sandy well enough. It was really rather difficult not to like him. He had chestnut hair and a lovely smile. Tall and slender, he looked sensational in his uniform, which only made Melinda more attracted to him. As Lily was prone to do more and more those days, she took her uneasiness to Brad Barton, who always seemed ready to share any of her concerns. He listened patiently and immediately understood why she felt as she did.

"Lily, I'm not certain what to tell you. Of course, an intimate relationship is strictly forbidden among staff and patients, but you and I both know that these sorts of liaisons are very common. It's impossible to think that so many men could be placed in these lovely surroundings, away from the horrors of war, tended to by lovely, innocent English maidens, and not expect there to be some affairs of the heart. You know it's bound to happen. Generally the resulting romances resolve themselves with nothing worse than a short-lived broken heart, until the next serviceman comes along. That isn't to say that what you're telling me doesn't concern me. I believe in this case I'll have a chat with the airman involved. Nothing terribly threatening, but enough to let him know that his behavior is frowned upon, and more so if he isn't serious about the young lady."

"Would you, Brad? I think that would serve the purpose. If he truly loves Melinda, that's one thing, but if this is simply a wartime romance, then it really must stop. All we need here at Claybourne Court is an unplanned baby born to an unmarried mother."

"Yes. I agree. I'll have a chat with him today. After I've spoken with him, I'll let you know. Perhaps we can have tea together this afternoon."

"That would be lovely, Brad. Why don't we meet in the library, where we can speak freely?"

They agreed upon the time, and Lily went about her day. She had appointments at her surgery and would plan on returning shortly before the appointed time.

⸎

Brad was not terribly encouraged by the conversation he had with Lieutenant St. John. The young airman said that he thought Melinda was a lovely girl, but that he was very near engagement to a girl back in Savannah, Georgia. He said he was a bit confused at the moment, as he truly had feelings for Melinda, but the difference in their cultures and upbringing concerned him. He felt certain that his parents would not be put off by her British background, but everyone in his town knew him and his family, as well as the "girl back home". He was sure he'd be treated as a pariah if he returned and said he intended to marry an English girl. He and Abigail, the young lady from Savannah, had known one another since childhood, and it had been assumed that they would marry when the time was right. Asked why he hadn't shared this information with Melinda, his face reddened and he stumbled around a bit before giving a clear answer.

"I find Melinda very attractive. I've been lonely since I arrived in England. She's been so good and kind to me. It would have been hard not to become entranced by her. I know that I should have made her aware of my situation at home, but I never seemed to find the proper time."

"Lieutenant, it appears you've found time for other things," Brad scowled. "Do you think it's fair to allow a young lady who is surely inexperienced with men, to give herself to you without knowing the entire truth about your intentions?"

"No, of course not. These things just happen, you know. Obviously, I need to tell her the entire truth."

"I hate to even speculate upon this, but what if Melinda Morris is already with child?"

"Oh god, sir. I would be in a rotten situation."

"You aren't saying that you would marry her under the circumstances?"

"Sir, I just don't know what I'd do. Aren't you getting ahead of yourself? There's been no talk about anything of that sort, has there?" he asked nervously.

"Not that I'm aware of, but surely you know it's not inconceivable. American boys coming over here and leaving unmarried girls alone to cope with being mothers is highly frowned upon."

"Yes, sir. I recognize that. Please, let's not even think about that at this juncture."

"All right, Lieutenant, I'm not going to continue on here. I hope you understand what I'm saying. Unless you have plans for marriage to this girl, I want to see it come to an end. If necessary, I can arrange to have you transferred to another recuperative facility."

"Yes, Colonel, I understand completely. I'll speak with Melinda, and tell her the entire truth. I'm sure once she hears what I have to say, she won't want anything more to do with me."

"I'm sorry, Lieutenant, but if we're to maintain order in this establishment there have to be rules to which we adhere."

"Yes, sir. I know that. Forgive me for forgetting that fact in the heat of passion. It won't happen again."

"I'm glad to hear that, Lieutenant St. John. All right, that's all. You're dismissed."

Sandy St. John went to his ward and lay down on the bed. He folded his arms under his head and thought at length. God he hated the conversation that was ahead of him. He truly did care for Melinda. If it hadn't been for Abigail, he would have seriously considered marriage to her. But, there *was* Abigail. Her parents were best friends to Sandy's parents. They were neighbors. He absolutely couldn't return from the war and tell her that their romance was over. No one would ever speak to him again. He would break her heart, as well as the hearts of both sets of parents. She was waiting for him back home and had been since the war began. The whole mess was an impossibility. What had he been thinking? The problem was he *hadn't* been thinking. He had simply acted on instinct. When "home" is thousands of miles away, with an ocean in between, everything connected with it seems remote. He *had* been lonely, and there was Melinda offering to plump his pillows, read to him, write letters, or just sit and talk, "chatting" as she called it, and he'd lost his head. But did he love her? Certainly he thought she was lovely. Creamy skin with high coloring, long nut-brown hair and immense blue eyes fringed with long lashes. She always seemed very calm and not easily excited. One could imagine coming home to her at the end of an arduous day. She was very much a port in a storm.

She was also intelligent. Her grammar was very proper, and he loved to hear her speak. But was that because he was in a foreign land, and the accent heightened her appeal? There was no question that she could be a passionate girl, and he was well aware that he had been her first. There was no question that she was in love with him. He turned over and hit the pillow with his fist. Damn. He was totally confused. Perhaps she would be willing to wait until he could return to the States, and speak to Abigail. He would know his true feelings so much better if he could spend some time with his American girl. But he knew it was highly unlikely that she would ever agree to that. He was simply going to have to tell the truth, and let the rest take care of itself.

He got up from the bed and limped over to the wall, where his cane stood. Then he began a search of the premises. He knew Melinda's hours and routine, so it wasn't difficult to find her. She was in the midst of making up a bed.

"Hello, Melinda. Aren't you due for a break?" he asked.

"Oh, is it that time already, Sandy? I've been working like a beaver ever since my arrival, scarcely had time for a breath. Yes, I'd love a break," she answered.

"Grab your cardigan, and let's take a short walk. I have some things I want to talk to you about," he said.

Melinda's heart soared. Was this what she had been waiting for? Was he going to propose? Her arms nearly shook as she put them into the sweater. She was saying a prayer to herself. She had never in her life felt this way about any man, and he had the power to make her the happiest person alive if what she suspected was true. They walked slowly down the stairway and out of the front door of the house. Then they turned to the left and moved in the direction of the pond, where there were benches upon which they could sit.

Once they arrived, they sat next to one another, and Sandy pitched a few pebbles into the water. There was silence between them, but finally he spoke.

"Melinda, we need to talk about us," he began.

"Us?" she answered. "What about us?"

"Well, you know how I feel about you, and I trust you feel the same about me."

"Yes, I think you could fairly say that," she smiled.

"It's just that there's a pretty big problem, Melinda."

"A problem? What sort of problem?" Her heart was racing. Were all of her dreams about to be dashed?

"I have a girl waiting for me back home," he answered straight away.

"What? You have a girl waiting for you at home? You mean in America? Do you mean she's waiting for you to come home and marry her?" Melinda's bottom lip had gone numb from shock. Why hadn't he told her before?

"Well, we aren't officially engaged yet. But we've known each other since we were very young. Our families are best friends. It's always been assumed that Abigail and I would end up married."

"Oh, Abigail. That's a pretty name," she said in a dazed voice. "So, are you telling me this now, so that I won't get any foolish ideas about wanting to marry you?"

"Melinda, I'm telling you because I'm terribly confused. The last thing I want to do is hurt you. I do mean it when I say I love you. But is it possible to be in love with two people at the same time? In a different way? I also love Abigail. Since I've met you, Abigail seems like a sister more than someone I want to marry."

"Oh," was all Melinda could think of to say. "I don't think I'm following you very well, Sandy."

"I know. I'm making an awful mess of this. I guess I'm trying to tell you that I don't know what I want until I've at least seen Abigail and had a chance to tell her in person what's happened."

"And you expect me to wait until the war is over and you get sent home, so that you can compare her to me and decide which of us will make you the happier?"

"Oh Melinda, no. That isn't what I mean. I just feel like I need to see her before I make such a life altering decision. I don't think it would be at all nice of me to just write her a letter telling her I'd met someone else. You wouldn't want me to do that to you, would you?"

"No, but I expect that's what you'll be doing, in a sense, when you write to me from America and tell me you've decided to stay with her."

"Oh God, Melinda, please try to understand. It isn't black and white. I wish it were."

"Sandy, I think it's really quite simple. You have made a commitment to Abigail, who has been counting on you since childhood. I've only known you a matter of months. It's war time. This happens to thousands of couples all of the time in war. It's the rare twosome who actually end up spending their lives together. Men go abroad, and they have these little flings, and then they return home and it's all forgotten. I shouldn't have been so foolish. But of course, I have no hold on you, and there's no question that we should no longer see one another. I'm not angry with you. I can understand how this could have happened. I only wish you had told me sooner, before I…. before we…. well, you know what I mean."

"Yes, I should have. Everything just happened so quickly. Please don't hate me."

"I don't hate you, Sandy. I could never hate you. Now please, just leave me alone for a bit. I need time to think. I don't intend to see you again. I do hope you're able to go home soon, and that you and Abigail will be very happy."

"Melinda – I – I don't know what to say. I hate leaving you like this."

"I know. But it's really the best way. Now please go. Please."

He got up and began to walk away from her. Then he stopped and gave her a long, searching look. "Will you be all right?" he asked.

"Yes, of course. I'm not a child. I've learned an important lesson, that's all. Goodbye then, Sandy, and take care of yourself."

15

In August, Sandy St. John was demobilized and sent back to America. His wound had rendered him neither fit to fly an airplane, nor to remain in the Armed Forces. Melinda didn't even say goodbye to him. Since their conversation in late June, they had avoided one another completely. Melinda had gone to Lily and had a good cry. Lily tried her best to provide comfort. A first broken heart was a frightfully painful thing. Melinda didn't want Sandy to know that she felt as though her heart had been torn out of her chest, and Lily promised that she would say nothing. Of course it was obvious by the expression on her face, and the sad, blank look in her eyes. Brad Barton saw it too, but there was nothing anyone could do. Both he and Lily were glad that the confused fellow hadn't strung her along. There would come a time when she would get over it and meet someone better suited to her, but that wasn't the sort of advice she was likely to want to hear at the moment. A girl never forgets her first love, her first real love.

Melinda was actually relieved when he left Claybourne Court. She no longer had to worry that she would run into him in the hallways or outside. Life returned to its rather boring routine, but it was better than being consumed with anxiety, knowing that he was still on the premises. However, the next happening was so frightful that she wasn't able to think straight. It took her back to Lily's arms on a warm day at the end of September. This time she made an appointment to see Lily her at the surgery, and the moment Dr. Claybourne saw Melinda's name in the appointment book, she knew exactly why she was paying a visit.

After an examination, Lily was proven correct. Melinda was three months pregnant. Of course it wasn't the first time in Lily's career that she'd dealt with such a problem. In fact it was quite common in the London hospital where she had trained. But Melinda was a friend, and her father was Lily's stepbrother. That made it a totally different affair. Melinda begged Lily not to tell her parents, and Lily had to abide by her wishes. The doctor-patient relationship was strictly confidential. If Melinda wished her parents to know, she would have to be the one to tell them. The same held true for Lieutenant St. John. Lily tried to accept the news calmly, as there was certainly no reason to cause Melinda further upset, but her heart ached for the sweet girl she had known since birth.

Melinda sat in Lily's office weeping uncontrollably. "What am I to do, Lily? This will kill my parents. I'll be an outcast in the village. How could I have been so stupid?"

Lily allowed time for the tears and self-recrimination, but finally she gently spoke to Melinda in a voice that made it clear it was time to stop being emotional and start thinking. Lily mentally went through a checklist in her mind, and then she began to present her thoughts out loud.

"Melinda, we have to think about options for you. I understand you're upset, but we have to think about what you intend to do. As I see it, you have two very broad choices that must be decided first. Everything else will flow from those decisions."

"All right," Melinda sniffed. "What do you think they are?"

"First, do you want to keep this baby? I mean keep it, raise it and devote yourself to being a mother? Or do you want to adopt it out?"

"Umm, is there any possibility I could consider a third option? I don't suppose since you're a doctor you would be willing to do an operation…well… you know…"

"Absolutely not, Melinda. That would be breaking the law, and my conscience wouldn't allow me to do such a thing. I understand why you would think of it. After all, it would be nice to blink your eyes and have this all go away. But it can't be done. And please don't even consider going to some back-alley butcher. I've seen the results of girls who've made that mistake. So I suggest we return to options one and two."

"What would you do?" Melinda asked.

"It doesn't matter what I'd do. This has to be your decision alone, and I think you need to make it before you ever speak to your parents. They will undoubtedly be like most parents and have an opinion one way or the other. You must have decided what you're going to do, and present it to them, firmly and decisively."

"I don't think I could carry a baby inside of me for nine months, give birth, and then give it away. Maybe if I was very poor and knew I had nothing to offer, but I can provide for a child. I have an income of my own, an inheritance from my grandparents. It isn't a fortune, but it's certainly enough to suffice. I'm not a little girl, Lily. After all, I'm nearly twenty-five years old. That is old enough not to have been so stupid," she said, as she burst into tears again.

"Melinda, you may be twenty-five, but age shouldn't always be counted in years. When it came to experience with this sort of thing, you were more on the order of sixteen. Unfortunately, I think the more experienced girls are the ones who don't find themselves in this position. But you are here now, and nothing can be done about it. Let me ask you one more question. What if you were to contact Sandy St. John and tell him what's happened? He didn't seem like a scoundrel to me. Don't you think he would return to England, and do his duty?"

"Oh, Lily. I don't want someone to marry me because it's his duty. If he truly loved me, he would have wanted to marry me and would have said so. We'd end up frightfully unhappy, and he would resent me all of his life. That would be no way for a child to grow up."

"You're probably correct. I suppose we can hope that he might contact you at some point, after he's had time to miss you and decide with certainty what he wants, but that can't be counted on. All right. Well, it sounds, then, like you're saying you want to have the baby and keep it?"

"Yes, I believe I am. But how would I go about it? I can't imagine walking around this village large with child, while everyone titters and laughs behind my back, as well as Mum and Dad's."

"I don't think most people are so cruel, Melinda, but I do agree. I think it might be best if you move to another place. You could go to one of the homes for unwed mothers. There are several in England, but I have to tell you, they aren't the most pleasant places. If possible, I'd rather not see you do that. Have you any relatives who live elsewhere? That would be a perfect solution, if the relative was kind and would take you in. Or you might move someplace else, where you can tell people that you're married, or better still, a war widow. We'll buy you a wedding band and have you lease a flat. Which of these sounds doable to you?"

"Oh Lord, I don't know, Lily. I haven't any relatives of the sort you describe. My Mum is an only child. You know my Dad's family. He had a brother who was killed in the Great War. I can't think of a single person, no cousins or the like. I absolutely don't want to go to one of those homes. I've heard horror stories. Generally, they want you to place the child for adoption, I think. I've hardly ever been anywhere. I've been to London a few times. Would it be too large a city for me to be on my own?"

"No, I don't think so. That's where I was during my medical school years. I rather enjoyed it, and Pia adored it. Of course, we were there under different circumstances. The up side would be that it's such a large city, the probability of anyone knowing your past would be very small. Plus, people just aren't as nosy in big cities. Another possibility would be to go and stay with Lady Cynthia and her second husband, Lord Belmont, at Belmont Hall. I think they'd be very nice about having you."

"Oh no. I don't think I could do that. Your mother-in-law always frightens me. I'm certain she would be judgmental. I like your first idea better."

"All right. Then we need to take steps in that direction. I'll go to London with you and help you find a place to live, and get you settled. Of course I'll visit regularly to make certain you're doing well, and I'll be there when the baby comes. After a bit, if you want to return to Claybourne-on-Colne, you could do so, when the child is older. You can say that you married in London and lost your husband in the war. I wish you could work at something, but I highly doubt that any employer would hire a woman who is expecting a child. We need to think of a reason why you've decided to move to London."

"Couldn't I say that my husband and I had lived in London prior to the war, but now that I'm expecting a child I'll need more room, so that prompted a relocation? It all sounds rather workable. I'm terrified, Lily, but I have to think about the baby. It doesn't matter about me. I have to do what's right for the baby."

"Yes, I think that explanation would work fine. But there are people who are bound to ask why you aren't with your parents, or another relation. So what explanation can there be for that?"

"Do you mean people here in the village, or London people?"

"Both, probably. But wait, Melinda. I just thought of something that would be less complex. I have a wonderful, dear friend who lives in London. I've known her since the Great War, when we nursed together in France. Her name was Madeline Brooks, but I call her Maddie. She married about ten years back, and her husband is an executive with the *London Times*. They're very dear people. They don't have any children. Maddie's surname is now Pettigrove. I know that if I contact her she'll tell you to come to them. She's wonderful, Melinda. In fact, your Mum and Dad even know her. She's come to Claybourne Court on numerous occasions. She was even an attendant in my wedding. Oh, she's the perfect answer, dear. Please say you'll agree to my ringing her. She and her husband will take you during the term of the pregnancy. She's a qualified nurse, which also makes it ideal. After the baby is born you can do as we discussed before, come back to Claybourne-on-Colne, if you want to, and explain that you were married to a soldier while in London, and that he was killed. What do you think?"

"Oh Lily, it does sound perfect. I'd feel a bit strange asking someone I don't even know to have me in her home and assume such responsibility. But, if you think she wouldn't object, I'd be eternally grateful to her."

"She won't object. Not Maddie. Then with your permission, I'm going to ring her. But no matter what she says, first you have to break the news to your parents. Please don't be frightened, Melinda. They're not babes in the woods. They love you and will do anything to help you. I think they'll be pleased that you want to keep the baby."

"I imagine they will. They love me dearly. I so hate disappointing them this way."

"I think you'll be surprised at how understanding they'll be. They're very fine people, and remember, I was there when you were just a tiny child. I've never known parents who loved their little girl more than they loved you. Of course, they still do."

"I know, Lily. I just never thought I'd disappoint them so."

"Melinda, it would be lovely if mothers and fathers could count on their children never doing anything at all to cause them worry. But, that isn't reality. Everyone on earth does something they wish they could take back, or redo. You'll just have to straighten your back now and tell them what's happened. At least you'll have a plan to present to them. Of course, Melinda, there's also the possibility that you'll decide to stay right here, have your baby, and tell anyone who has a bad attitude to 'bugger off'," Lily laughed.

She knew very well that Melinda wouldn't opt for such a choice, but Lily wanted to make sure she'd presented all possibilities.

"No, Lily. I think the idea of going to London is best by far. I'll be fine. Do you suppose I could get a job, just so that I could keep my mind occupied?"

"Maddie works for the Red Cross. I'd be surprised if they don't jump at the chance to take on anyone who wishes to volunteer. With your background, helping recuperating military men at Claybourne Court, I'm certain there would be ample opportunity for you to use the skills you've developed, at least until you're further along in your pregnancy."

"Yes. I'd like that. I'd feel useful. And Lily, what name shall I give for my husband? Would it be completely wrong for me to use Sandy's name?"

"Well, he *is* the father after all, isn't he? A lot depends on if you intend to tell your child who the father is. If so, then I would think his name should be on the birth certificate"

"Don't you think every child has a right to know who they are? I wouldn't feel good about not letting my child know about his or her father."

Lily immediately thought of Pia, who hadn't known until she was sixteen who her father was. There was no question in Lily's mind about how she felt. "Yes, Melinda, that's what I believe, but everyone has a right to decide for themselves."

"Sandy's name will be on the birth register. But shall I also *tell* people that my husband's name was St. John?"

"I don't think that's feasible. If you intend to bring the baby back here eventually, so many people knew about Sandy. No one will see the birth record, but I think you'd be wise to pick a different surname. It's very unlikely that anyone you meet would know him in London. But just the opposite is true here. I don't think you need to go into great detail. People will understand if you don't feel like going on about him."

"Yes. All right. Did you tell me that your friend Maddie's name is Pettigrove? Perhaps I could use that name, as a sort of tribute to her."

"Well... you would need to have Maddie's permission. I think she would agree, but I'm not certain it's the best choice. Again, people here know Maddie. They also know you aren't related to Maddie. You'd have to make your husband a relation to Maddie's husband. I think it's getting too complex. Why not say your husband's name was Samuel Paulson? My other friend from the VAD was killed in the Blitz. Her name was Poppy Paulson. Her husband was also taken. You could use that surname because it's common enough. And Samuel is close enough to Sanford, so you'd probably get used to it rather easily. You know, Sammy and Sandy?"

"Yes. Right. I just want to make certain I haven't forgotten anything. When will we go to London?"

"As soon as you've told your parents, and I've cleared it with Maddie. Your parents might want to come along with us."

"I'll have to chat with them tonight. Oh, how I dread the thought. But I can do it. I'll tell them right after supper, and then I'll ring you."

"All right then. We have a plan. It's going to be all right, Melinda. I'll ring Maddie after my appointments are finished today. Now, I have a patient waiting, so I shall have to speak with you later. Do ring me tonight. And don't be frightened. Your parents are wonderful people."

Lily, along with Melinda and Jane Morris, traveled to London two days later. As Lily had suspected, Jane was loving and kind, and only said she would do everything in the world to help her daughter. She agreed with the plan that had been arranged. Both she and David said they would pay Melinda's expenses. They wanted to make certain Maddie lived in a nice, safe neighborhood. Lily and Jane talked at length after Melinda broke the news to them, and it was a relief to know that their thoughts were akin to one another. Melinda's parents weren't angry with her, and were only saddened that she couldn't have married the man she obviously adored.

When Maddie learned of Melinda's predicament, she immediately said, "Send her to me, Luv." Lily had known that would be the response. Maddie had always been the most open-minded of the three girls she'd met at Aubigny in France, and Lily knew she wasn't about to be judgmental toward Melinda. "There but for the grace of God go I," she said. "The poor girl must be heartbroken. Don't worry, Lily. She'll be loved and cared for. Henry will be a dear. You know I would never have married a priggish man. He'll treat her with respect and kindness. When do you want her to make the move?"

"As soon as possible, Maddie. She's three months, and slim as a willow, but that can and will change. I'd like to see her settled, and out of Claybourne-on-Colne very soon."

"How does the day after tomorrow sound? I'll tidy a room and make it welcoming. Shall we say sometime in the afternoon? I'll talk to Henry tonight, but that won't be any hurdle."

"Maddie, you're an angel. Thank you so much. I know you'll love Melinda. She's very sweet. I can't imagine that she'll be any problem for you. She's a quiet girl and will undoubtedly keep mostly to herself. I'm going to make certain she has a wedding ring to go along with the story of a husband who is missing in action. She prefers that to his being deceased, thinks it's less of a lie."

"Well, he certainly *is* missing, isn't he?" She laughed. "I know it isn't funny, Lily, but sometimes if one doesn't look for humor in a situation, it becomes even more unbearably grim. Tell her that we truly look forward to having her with us and that she's not to worry about anything."

When Lily passed the news on to Melinda, she was greatly relieved. The entire plan had fallen into place with relative ease, and now it was only a matter of putting it into action. Edward, the Claybourne Court chauffeur, drove them to London. Maddie and Henry lived in a lovely Victorian townhouse in Chelsea. Sadly, bombing was still occurring, and poor Melinda would have to get used to the wail of air-raid sirens. After Lily and Pia's ordeal, no one took for granted that they couldn't become victims. But the house was in a safer area than some, and Melinda didn't seem overly concerned. The war had gone on for so long that most had become accustomed to the inconveniences and precautions that had to be taken. Melinda handed her ration book over to Maddie the moment they met. Maddie laughed and thanked her, saying that it was amazing how the world had changed. "Once, when people came to visit, they were offered lovely cakes and tea. Now they immediately supply the hostess with a rationing book."

Melinda and Maddie immediately took to one another, which didn't surprise Lily. Both had kind, gentle personalities. Maddie hugged her warmly and never said a word about the reason for her stay, except that she was delighted to have her and wanted Melinda to feel completely at home. Maddie had prepared a cozy room for her, with a fireplace and casement windows that looked out on the garden. She also showed her where they intended the nursery would be, right next to Melinda's bedroom. There was a cook and housekeeper, but the way of life in the Pettigrove home seemed quite informal. Melinda's father brought her trunk up the stairs, and they both exclaimed over the beautiful accommodations. Melinda was overwhelmed at Maddie's generosity and expressed her appreciation over and over.

"It's what I would have wanted someone to do for me, Luv. Henry and I are going to enjoy having you with us, and when the baby arrives, we'll love it like it's ours. Don't mistake me. I'm not about to usurp your position as its mother," she laughed. "But, it will be fun to have a little one about, at least for a time. You're welcome to stay as long as you want."

When it came time for her parents and Lily to return to Claybourne-on-Colne, Melinda became a bit teary-eyed, but Maddie was a jewel and told her that she could ring her parents anytime she felt the need. In turn, they promised to visit London frequently. As they drove away, Melinda stood on the walk waving, her golden wedding ring sparkling in the sun.

16

The autumn and winter passed faster than Melinda would have dared hope. Her parents traveled to London for Christmas, and Maddie graciously played hostess. Melinda was six months gone, and she was no longer the slim, willowy lady she'd been upon arrival. Wagers were being taken on whether the child would be a boy or a girl. Like all others, Melinda just hoped for a healthy baby. In her heart of hearts, she leaned toward a little girl, only because she couldn't imagine raising a little boy without a father. She was also concerned about whether she should name the baby after its father if it was a boy. Many men, of course, liked their sons to be named for them, but this was a completely different situation. The chances of Sandy ever knowing his first-born child were remote. He would surely marry, if he hadn't already, and when a legitimate son was born, he very well could be his father's namesake. Melinda didn't feel right about there being two children from the same father with identical names. She decided that she would leave the honor of continuing the family line with a 'junior', up to Sandy's true wife. Anyway, she had already discussed all of that with Lily, and knew that she couldn't return to Claybourne-on-Colne with a baby named Sandy. If the baby were a girl, she had decided upon Annabel.

The war continued to rage on, with action in Italy, Russia, and Africa. More and more battles were being won by the Allied forces, but the Germans showed no sign of weakening their resolve. Clay Marshall continued to prowl the skies in his new Spitfire, with more and deeper sorties into German occupied territory. Win was almost exclusively occupied with practice landings on beaches, with the clear knowledge that there was obviously a planned offensive of enormous importance given the time that was being dedicated to its preparation. Of course, no one had the slightest idea exactly what they were preparing for, or where it would be. At one point he was ordered to Scotland, where he was introduced to a new sort of landing craft. It was a solid guess that this was about to be used in whatever was being planned. Rumors abounded, but nobody knew anything with certainty. Those who did weren't saying. Win was promoted to captain, making it a certainty that he would lead a platoon in whatever lay ahead.

London was by no means forgotten during that period. While the Blitz had ended, there was still bombing, not only in London but throughout England, particularly in the larger cities. Melinda became used to spending entire nights in the Anderson shelter, and the sirens no longer sent her reeling from fear. More often than not, the bombs didn't fall anywhere near Chelsea. All along it had been the East End that got the worst of it, although even Buckingham Palace hadn't been safe from the Nazis. A bomb had hit the palace as far back as September, 1940, while the King and Queen were in residence. Their bravery had greatly endeared them to the British people. They only left London to visit their two children at Windsor on weekends.

On March 2, 1943, the same day that the Germans began a withdrawal from Tunisia, Africa, Annabel Morris Paulson was born at St. Stephens Hospital in Chelsea. Melinda's parents were there, and so was Lily, along with Maddie and Henry Pettigrove. Lily wasn't able to handle the delivery, since she didn't have staff privileges at St. Stephens, but she was accorded the honor of being able to attend the birth since she was a registered physician. Melinda did not have a bad time of it. Labor lasted about seven hours, and the baby was quite tiny, just a little over five pounds. She was very pretty, with quite a lot of chestnut hair and a dainty rosebud mouth. Everybody fell madly in love with her, and though it wasn't said, there were silent prayers of gratitude that Melinda had made the decision to keep the little girl. The only sadness Melinda felt was the knowledge that Annabel's father wasn't there to see his child. But she had grown used to knowing she would never see him again, and her full attention was placed upon his offspring.

The decision was made that Melinda and Annabel would remain in London for perhaps a little over a year. By that time, when she returned to Claybourne-on-Colne, it would make perfect sense that she had met a soldier while he was on furlough in London, had married quickly, as happened frequently, and learned she was going to have a child shortly after that. Then, according to the story, he went missing and she'd heard nothing since. It wasn't an uncommon story, and no one knew how often it was actually true. It did seem that soldiers had a propensity for ensuring that their gene pool survived on the eve of battle.

❧

During the summer months there was heavy fighting in Italy, and the British carried out a massive air raid on Hamburg in Germany, causing a huge firestorm. On September 8, Italy's government surrendered, and in October the new government declared war on Germany. Yet the Germans fought on. Daylight raids on their country caused horrific damage, but Hitler refused to even consider that the Nazis might lose. After all, they still had France.

Annabel grew and thrived. Melinda was eager to take her back to her home village and show her off to everyone. But she kept to her prearranged schedule, counting the days until the summer of 1944.

Her parents visited as often as possible and adored their little granddaughter. She fast became the light of their lives. Maddie and Henry were equally enamored with her, and although Maddie was forty-eight, she and Henry decided that they wished to adopt a war orphan. They knew the chance of getting a small baby was remote, but any child at all would be welcome. By the time Melinda was packing her belongings, they were thrilled to welcome a little seven-year- old girl into their midst. Her name was Grace, and both parents had been lost during the Blitz. Melinda having lived with them for over a year had a profound impact on Maddie and Henry's lives, preparing them for sharing their home and their lives with a child.

Jordan had turned eighteen in August of 1943, and nothing Lily could say or do kept him from enlisting in the military. She had promised that she wouldn't hold him back, and she was a woman of her word. He joined the British Expeditionary Forces and trained as a paratrooper. Lily loathed the idea of two sons and a son-in-law being in the face of danger, but it was the patriotic thing, and she couldn't begrudge his wanting to do his bit for England. She had so hoped that the miserable war would have ended by 1943, but that wasn't to be. Jordan was sent to a military station in Essex, and Lily added his name to the list of soldiers she prayed for nightly. By the spring of 1944, Jordan was a well-trained parachutist.

Melinda arrived back in Claybourne-on-Colne in April of 1944. Her arrival coincided with a brief furlough that was given to both Clay and Win. Pia was over-the-moon at seeing her husband for the first time in quite a long spell. They spent the majority of their time ensconced in the Dower House, while Lily temporarily moved back into the Great House, where Win was likewise cocooned with Susie. The family enjoyed each other at meal times, and for brief spells outside to enjoy the lovely spring weather. Brad Barton was practically a member of the family by then and joined them whenever possible. The war had changed so many things in everybody's lives, and it was hard to imagine that Claybourne Court would ever return to a normal, peaceful country house. What had begun as a conflict that many predicted would never even be a real war, had become a never ending exchange of death and destruction.

After their husbands returned to their posts, there was despondency. Pia and Susie wondered if their lives would always consist of short visits from their spouses, interspersed with long separations filled with continual worry. During such a gloomy time, Melinda couldn't help but think to herself that perhaps she was fortunate not to have a husband. Annabel was enough for her, and while she wished with all of her heart that her little girl could have been raised with her daddy, she was grateful that Annabel did have a loving family with Melinda and her grandparents. David and Jane Morris had always been highly thought of in the village, and everyone took to their sweet granddaughter. Therefore Melinda and Annabel Paulson were a welcome addition to Claybourne-on-Colne.

Over a two week period the beds at Claybourne Court's recuperative hospital began to quickly fill with patients who were being discharged from London area hospitals. Colonel Brad Barton had an inkling that the sudden influx of new admissions meant that there was something big in the offing, some military action of major proportion. It was the only thing that made sense. When there were suddenly large numbers of new patients, it generally meant that beds were being opened in the expectation of casualties being brought into the hospitals which treated the severely wounded.

He wasn't wrong. Over several days leading up to June 6, 1944, a massive number of troops were gathered along the southern coastline. Win was moved to a camp about five miles from Tilbury. Similarly, Jordan was moved to a tented camp near Southampton. On June 5, Clay Marshall was piloting one of five thousand British planes that dropped more than five thousand tons of bombs across the English Channel, along the French coastline, to knock out enemy encampments. The stations were sealed off and no one in England knew that the greatest battle of the war would take place on June 6. Win sat in his tent, smoking one cigarette after another, having been briefed on the plan, but still not certain of the location. He was stunned when Winston Churchill himself strolled up to him with a large cigar in his mouth, shook his hand, and wished him good luck. Win's emotions careened from being certain he was going to die, to feeling positive that the Allied troops were going to be victorious. Jordan Claybourne was nervous and terrified. It would be the first action he had seen in the war. He thought of his father, and the bravery he'd heard about all of his life; he thought of his older brother and wished he could be serving under his leadership. He said a silent prayer for his brother-in-law and regretted not having joined the RAF.

Then everything happened at once. Win was crammed into the bowels of a ship and given a bag to use for sea sickness, while Jordan was loaded onto an airplane and strapped into his parachute. The largest amphibious action ever to occur in the history of war was upon them. By nightfall Win was firmly ensconced above a Normandy beach, and Jordan lay with a bullet through his forehead in the hills not far away. Clay Marshall was still in his 'office', the cockpit of his Spitfire, weary but unharmed. By the next morning all of England would know about the success of their mission. Lily Claybourne was devastated at the loss of her youngest son while relieved that her eldest had come through. Pia was biting her nails, waiting to hear news about her husband. Susie Claybourne felt joy at the knowledge that her husband had survived, but grief that her young brother-in-law, Jordan Claybourne, would never return from his first battle.

Many men from their small village were either lost or injured that day, but when the news came just a month and a half later that Paris had been liberated on August 25, the people of Britain knew that their husbands, sons, brothers and sweethearts hadn't died, or suffered, in vain.

It still took almost another full year, until May 8, 1945, for Adolph Hitler to admit that his grand design had failed. On that day, Victory in Europe was declared, and nearly all the world rejoiced. Lily Claybourne wept with pent-up emotion, sorrow and past memories when she heard the news. Colonel Bradley Barton put his arms round her, and holding her close to his heart, asked her to be his wife. She accepted his proposal immediately. She would end her life as Lily Barton once again. The journey had been long. She prayed that there would be no more war in her lifetime. Brad planned on leaving the military, having earned a well-deserved retirement. They would remain at Claybourne Court and would travel extensively.

Melinda Paulson was shocked when Sandy St. John returned to England on the first passenger ship to arrive from America. He boarded a crowded train to Claybourne-on-Colne. There, he returned to Melinda and met his tiny daughter for the first time. Abigail had not been the one, but he'd wanted to tell Melinda in person. Although David and Jane Morris didn't necessary like the idea that their daughter would be marrying and moving to America, they couldn't possibly begrudge her happiness. Annabel's birth certificate would show the proper name of Melinda's husband.

Jordan was buried in the vast military cemetery at Normandy, under one of the thousands of white crosses that marked the place where they had fallen. It was nearly in the sight of the White Cliffs of Dover. Pia and Clay bought a quaint cottage in Claybourne-on-Colne. Clay also left the Royal Air Force, and for a spell they planned to enjoy one another and the country life they both enjoyed. Later he would investigate employment as a commercial pilot. John and Gena Garrett adopted a war orphan, and Gena once again returned to the job she loved best, being a wife and mother.

Later when Lily Barton pondered the journey that had been her life, she realized that, after all was said and done, she and her loved ones had made a difference for their country.

OTHER BOOKS BY MARY CHRISTIAN PAYNE

The Somerville Trilogy

Willow Grove Abbey: Book 1 of the Somerville Trilogy
St. James Road: Book 2 of the Somerville Trilogy
Serendipity: Book 3 of the Somerville Trilogy

The Claybourne Trilogy

The White Feather: Book 1 of the Claybourne Trilogy
The White Butterfly: Book 2 of the Claybourne Trilogy
White Cliffs of Dover: Book 3 of the Claybourne Trilogy

The Thornton Trilogy

No Regrets: Book 1 of The Thornton Trilogy
No Gentleman: Book 2 of the Thornton Trilogy
No Secrets: Book 3 of the Thornton Trilogy

ABOUT THE AUTHOR

Mary Christian Payne was highly successful in several management positions in Fortune 500 Companies, in New York City, St. Louis, Missouri, Orlando Florida, and Tulsa, Oklahoma. Her work included Grant writing, and designing and writing Training Manuals for Executive Training Programs.

She left the corporate world, and became Director of Career Development at the Women' Resource Center at the University of Tulsa, where she designed a program that enabled hundreds of adult women to return to college and better their lives. She received the Mayor's Pinnacle Award in 1993 for this achievement. Mary left that position when the Center closed, and then opened her own Career Counseling Center. She retired in 2008.

Mary Christian Payne became a successful, best-selling author at the age of 71, with the help of her publisher, Tom Corson-Knowles. All of her life, she had wanted to write, and had received accolades for her unpublished work. She was encouraged in college, and writing was a significant part of the various jobs she held.

In 2013, she read Tom Corson-Knowles' book about publishing on Kindle. She wrote to him and he telephoned her. The rest is history. Since that time, she has published nine books, with more on the way.

Mary lost her husband in June, 2015, after 33 years of marriage. The grief process brought a lull to her writing, but she found that putting words on paper helped immensely. She is now in the process of writing her second novel since his death. She lives in Tulsa, Oklahoma, with her two beloved Maltese dogs.

Sign up for the newsletter to get news, updates and new release info from Mary Christian Payne:

http://bit.ly/MaryChristianPayne

One Last Thing...

If you enjoyed this book, I'd be very grateful if you'd post a short review on Amazon. Your support really does make a difference and I read all the reviews personally.

Thanks again for your support!